A VOID IN YOU

Gerardo Suarez

A Void In You
Copyright © 2022 by Gerardo Suarez

All rights reserved. No part of this publication may be reproduced, distributed, or transmitted in any form or by any means, including photocopying, recording, or other electronic or mechanical methods, without the prior written permission of the publisher, except in the case brief quotations embodied in critical reviews and other noncommercial uses permitted by copyright law.

ISBN: 978-1-63945-414-3 (Paperback)
            978-1-63945-415-0 (Ebook)

The views expressed in this book are solely those of the author and do not necessarily reflect the views of the publisher, and the publisher hereby disclaims any responsibility for them.

Writers' Branding
1800-608-6550
www.writersbranding.com
orders@writersbranding.com

Contents

Move Forward v

Delectables Bar. June 7th, 2013 1

My Home. June 8th, 2013 9

My Home. June 21st, 2013 15

My Home, July 12th 2013 23

A Cafe called "Something Sweet", August 5th, 2013 27

Serenity's Birthday. September 4th, 2013 31

The Buffet Bar, February 7th, 2014 45

Bisbee. Sunday March 2nd, 2014 59

My Home. May 29th, 2014 65

An Unknown time, Months and Months later 67

My Home, February 5th, 2015 69

April 4th, 2015 77

Move Forward

Inevitably it led to disaster. On five separate occasions it happened. On five uniquely scattered days interspersed within the timeline of countless months we met, locked side by side in the fascination of my imagination, inseparable but torn apart. In the five days of our meetings, I was systematically shut down like an old, defeated man trying to stay alive long enough to make a difference. Her name: Samantha.

I can no longer look at that name in peace.

Delectables Bar. June 7th, 2013

And in the first light, the world is covered in a false darkness that can reveal its surroundings over time.

I honestly just wanted a different scene. Something I was used to, somewhere I could ignore my surroundings in my own way and not feel overrun by country music. The wannabe country boys and girls that were dressed in the attire because it was trending annoyed me. I'm not one to judge but when attire becomes an issue with respect, and the ego inflates because of it, that particular attire is not for you. Despite the trend and how girls wear those small, bare-assed shorts, only some girls could pull it off, the rest weren't so lucky, but they would never admit it.

It was the evening of my friends' friend birthday party and Count-Ricks' was the destination, a country bar that held and still holds no appeal for me. But, I was invited and after being single for a while I figured what the hell? I can at least try a country themed bar, never been to one and I should at least be fair, something my ex never considered.

Not even half an hour into the meet n greets with everyone and the birthday girl and this bar was already too damn much. The line coiled around the establishment, and I was not in the proper attire for apparently THIS was the night you should have dressed up. I could not stand everyone and their fake- ass "Cuun-tree" accents and, above all, those who could drink with me had to drive. It seemed like it would be a regular shit.

We waited in line for what seemed to be forever while time was wasting away, and the anticipation of an awesome night faded faster than the growing disbelief that set in once I heard of the cover charge:

"25 dollars please."

What the fuck? I had never seen nor foolishly paid a more obscene cover charge. Could it be a deposit for something better or is this paying their damn bills? Only time would tell, it just couldn't tell me soon enough. They knew this night was special. Well, it wasn't, it was just a Friday, and I'm sure SOMETHING came up thus making everyone want to come out. That was an understatement.

"OK everyone, let's find a spot! Keep an eye out!" said the bday girl. Who is she again?

In reality, that was useless. Inebriated people filled the establishment from the entrance to the end of the room, all trying to leave their mark on the night and pretending to be whoever they wanted to be.

I did my best to enjoy the surroundings, but everyone dispersed, some into the crowd, others to their group or one of the three bars serving drinks. I figured I should take the advantage of the only reason I was here, beer for only one-dollar. Of course they were not what I expected; beer served in water cups? That's a recipe for an unfortunate and memorable shitty drinking experience. With one ridiculous expensive cover charge, beer served in cups meant for children and a drink made in haste; I decided it was time to create my party.

For about 5 minutes, I asked myself if this was a place I wanted to stay in. That's all it took, just five minutes and Twenty-five dollars before I decided to leave this place. The truth was I decided on leaving this place since I learned what it was. I leaned over to my friend Carson as we stood near the bar; perhaps he was the only other sane one besides me who saw that this place was not somewhere we wanted to be.

"Carson, you having fun?"

"No." Do you ever?

"Good, let's go."

We dodged everyone on our way to the exit. The damn place was an ever-shifting maze of drunken bastards and bad judgment. We made it to the taxi line and while I already hailed a cab, Carson was missing. I called immediately, fearing the meter was running. There was no answer.

I thought to text him and after several messages, it would be easier for me to go without him, and he could meet me on 4th Avenue. I waited for perhaps seven minutes until he came from the doors, happier than I've ever seen him.

"Dude, I was talking to this girl." He climbed in the car and closes the door.

"And? Did you get her number?"

"No, but I talked to her."

"And when will you be talking to her again?"

He sat in silence, the kind of silence a child gives when their mother talks down to them for failing to do something so simple.

"That's what I thought." Poor boy doesn't know how to close. Poor boy hasn't had a girlfriend. I don't think he even knows what a girl is.

"Where to boys?" The taxi driver asked.

"4th avenue, anywhere on 4th Avenue," I replied as we pulled away seeing the Count-Ricks's lights fade in the distance. Perhaps it was a bit of tiredness from using up so much energy trying to make a doomed night better. Or perhaps because I knew I was going to make it all work in the end, even if there were only five or six hours of nightlife left.

"Bad day?"

"Trying to make a boring day better."

We drove for a good thirty minutes while I learned a bit of our taxi driver, Linda. She was the sweetest woman I had ever met, and she was determined to help us rekindle the evening. We arrived at our destination, and one particular place caught my attention because of the unique light designs on the walls. Various party lights were projecting geometric patterns and fog machines giving the illusion of waterfalls that lead into the nothingness.

"Thank you, Linda."

"My pleasure hun. You two stay safe now!"

We made our way inside; my eyes enticed by the cool blue light dancing on the walls and floor, changing color every few seconds. I knew this was a place I could to stay for a while; this was all I needed. Little did I know I got so much more than I could have expected.

She sat at the bar, her two friends around her with a third talking to my buddy. I had only known Carson for two months, and I couldn't stand his outlook on life, not because it was dark or too cheerful, but because it was one-tracked. "Cars" this and "Cars" that, his idea of flirting was trying to see what's under the hood, literally. He wasn't a bad guy, but he wasn't someone who could hold meaningful conversations. He was lonely and quite frankly, so was I. But I wouldn't talk about myself right off the bat. Hell, I hated talking about myself unless there was a lesson in the end.

Regardless, he was hitting it off with a girl neither of us knew. She wasn't my type, and her voice was something out of a cartoon. Imagine that in your ear, a squeaky nearly helium-driven voice with a laugh that could blow out your eardrum. For about twenty-five minutes they hit it off; he was talking about whatever he loved and she with whatever she loved. It would seem they are a match made for themselves and only themselves. But I digress.

As I finished my third of fourth dirty Shirley I saw her, in a way eyeballing me. Carson wasn't going to finish anytime soon, and I was getting tired of the two talking to mirrors. This girl took my friend I was going to take her friends. They weren't too far from me, just three stools away. Sitting on that stool was what sent me down a path I might never have of known and changed me slowly and with each lesson that came with it, I lost a bit of my reality.

I sat across from her. "My name is Samantha," she said; drink in her hand, a beautiful pair of eyes focused on me. That was a first. "And I'm Jerry." It wasn't the alcohol talking, not even once except when I mentioned half way through our shotgun introductions, which is the element of their choice, and why. One said wind, two said fire and one said earth, me, I was the Avatar, master of all four elements. Cheering commenced.

I could have started with my name as I introduced myself to them all, but what fun was that? Intrigue people I always say. Don't make yourself known to just anyone. I had never been to this bar before, and the timing seemed right, as I had ditched a friend of a friend's birthday two hours earlier. My first time there was already my last.

We spent the duration of the evening at the bar, talking about our dreams and hopes, our fears and our pet peeves, our shit jobs and how we would love to have an elemental power. I must have bought six or seven dirty Sherries that night, the most vodka I have had in a long time since beer is usually my drink of choice. I was enjoying the night so much that I felt the glass I was using should become part of the group.

As our last calls were ordered and shot glasses thrown back, I decided to take the glass with me while exiting the establishment, carefully walking down the street happily buzzed, to get a taxi. Just as I though the night would close, an idea emerged. I was starving and with the copious amounts of alcohol in my system, I knew my morning was going to be less than plentiful. "Hey, you guys hungry?" I asked as a deluge of people oversaturated the streets.

I got a few mixed answers with only three of the six saying yes, me not included. I received a yes from Carson, an unfortunate yes from Mimi and a yes from Samantha, the most wanted yes of them all. I still don't remember what happened to the other two.

"There is an IHOP by my place on Silverbell and Grant. It's an easy ride from here."

"I know of one even closer, we can go there."

"Alright, well, if that's the case lets go."

"Cool! See you boys there."

All I needed to know was that Carson had enough money since we would eventually need a ride home from a taxi. Depending where the location of the IHOP Samantha suggested we needed to make sure we could at least get home. We made our way across the street to reach the taxi lane. At that moment, Carson said something that goes against even the most sophisticated rules of The Code of Bro; he became an obnoxious prick.

"Jerry. Jerry. Jerry. Listen to me." He cannot hold his alcohol.

"What is it man? You OK?"

"Listen, Samantha was the hottest girl we talked to all night and I noticed that you two were hitting it off… Do you like her?"

I was unsure how to respond considering that Sam and I had JUST met a few hours ago. Truth was, I did find her attractive, but there was nothing helping that thought. I didn't know what she thought. I didn't even know if she had a boyfriend.

"I find her attractive, yes. Why?"

"Because man, I'm warning you, if you don't get with her, I WILL. If you need me to play wingman, I will. I will lie to her for you. But I WILL get with her if you don't."

I cannot condone his actions for he was not of sound mind. All I could say to myself in that instance was he is no one to be self-indulged.

"Alright man, thanks." IF he weren't my friend and neighbor, I would have left him on the spot.

Not three steps on our way to the taxis when we hear two guys coming up the street yelling at each other, ready to fight. Carson had the brilliant idea to try to step in and stop the ordeal, not knowing he was a toothpick compared to these guys. The two men were arguing in an unintelligible drunken language while their friends were trying to keep them apart. I was happily enjoying the melee as Carson started to approach them. 'I can stop them.' He muttered. My only thought was 'No, you cannot.' The two men were pulled apart before anything serious could happen. We finally got our cab. I drunkenly typed the address on my GPS, just to help the cab driver, even though I was sure he knew how to get there.

We reached the destination, and the girls were sitting happily in their booth, menus up, waters out, and hot chocolate partially drank. It didn't take long for me to order; the house burger with a fried egg on top and barbecue sauce with seasoned fries and a Dr. Pepper. I'm disgusting. Before the food came, I noticed Samantha had a bowl of whip cream. I thought it might be for pancakes but as she stuffed a spoonful in her mouth, I realized that wasn't the case.

"Really? Whip cream just like that?"

She smiled and like a reflex that is so natural that one doesn't even know it's happening; she tried to speak only to have a spoonful of whip cream instead.

"(Unintelligible noise of pure passion from stuffing her face with a spoonful of whip cream)."

"Hmm, welp, it's not like it's a gross thing."

We laughed it off, her and I as if we were the only two people in the entire restaurant. I could see the look on Mimi's face, the face of pure agony. She seemed as if she was trying to find any excuse to talk to us, even for a minute to break the uninteresting web Carson had created. The food came and, of course, talking ceased. After all, we were all starving and quite buzzed. The remarkable part was that Samantha, with her beautiful physique and natural beauty, downed an entire appetizer sampler and, strangely enough, a second bowl of whip cream.

Even before we agreed to come to IHOP, I already had the idea in the back of my mind as to how we were supposed to get back. I had mentioned to Carson on the way over to IHOP how much money he had with him. For me, I normally carry forty dollars in cash with my debit card for use only as a last resort. By the end of the night, I had about fifteen dollars left and my bank account was happy I didn't go all out. I hated going all out.

"Carson, you have enough for the ride home?"

Before he could even answer, Samantha immediately offered to take us home. While I couldn't flat out take the offer since I knew she lived so far away, I was happy she asked.

"Are you sure? You live far away, and we're at the end of the west side, past the freeway."

"Did I stutter? Haha, yes, I'll take you two. Let's finish up soon, I have work in the morning."

We finished our food, stomachs full and wallets happy. The buzz that taunted me with a possible headache disappeared as the tiny food soldiers went into my body and defeated the army of alcohol that hadn't dissolved into my bloodstream. Today was a good day. The night was the best night I could have.

The ride back home was different. I couldn't remember the last time that I had ridden in the back of a car after a night of drinking even though it happened several more times, let alone from a girl I had just met. I must admit, I was rather tired from the evening as the alcohol and food found the middle ground and decided to call it a truce, engulfing me with a wave of sleepiness. Samantha was still lively even after it all, Mimi was still there, and Carson was drifting in and out of sleep. His bigger-than-normal head gave a rather amusing display of balance as the car shifted on the way home.

Before long, Samantha had asked if there were any requests for music or if we had any music to play. I would have offered my phone, but my music is less than what normal people listen to for I enjoy metal. I enjoy the band Cradle of Filth. While it would get a bad rep from ANYONE who cannot understand the complexities of this particular band, I looked at their lyrics in the form of artwork. Poetry in every line, unique sounds in ever track. Carson however offered his phone immediately.

"I have one!" You don't have to scream, bro.

"Alright, which one?"

"Just plug in and play, you'll all love it."

While I expected a song about cars or how to train your car or, god forbid, how to take your car on the proper date to ensure a healthy motor, his song of choice was not disappointing. He had chosen a song performed by Lindsey Sterling he titled 'dubstep violin'. The beats mixed with the violin and created magnificent music. I looked her up while we drove home.

Car ride's always seem longer when you aren't driving or when you failed to call shotgun. Conversation is what moves time on any journey. While I couldn't talk to anyone on the ride home as easily as I wanted to, at least the sounds of new music saw to my enjoyment, adding to a rather interesting and unexpected night.

We finally made it to our homes, and while I would have done whatever I could to shake off the sleepiness and talk to Samantha longer, it was an impossible task. She was sleepy, Mimi was being the toddler repeating that she wanted to go home, and Carson was about to pass out on the street. We simply waved goodbye as she exclaimed that we should do this again soon. I had one butterfly in my stomach simply because I thought she was beautiful and getting to know her a little throughout the night was something I had not experienced in a long time. Carson however saw to ruin my moment.

"Thanks for the night, maaaaaan."

"Yeah man." Glad I invited you…

"Good night my friend. Remember, get her or I will."

He turned and left without another word. It's amusing watching those who cannot hold their alcohol because whatever they say is always a stitch and in the morning, they swear you will hold it against them. I know for I'm no stranger to the regrets of the morning *I'm Sorry, Eli*. Luckily, it wasn't me this time. I could have been mad at Carson. I shouldn't have been though. Why? Because I knew that although we are neighbors, tonight would be the last night I would ever see him again.

My night ended with a baffling thought, a full stomach, and a nice hot shower. I messaged my thank you to Samantha and hoped she was telling the truth about doing this again. But I had a better idea.

My Home. June 8th, 2013

The Uncertainties of the present can hinder the imagination of the future.

I took a chance and decided to invite her to hang out again, this time, not drunk at 3am with that fuckhead Carson and especially not with Mimi. Today, it would be her and me, just us, getting to know each other. I mentioned I had a few errands to run, nothing major and considering her commute; I would drive us for the duration of the day. She came to my place in her white Golf GT, a cute little thing that was remarkably still in working order. She called. I loved her assertiveness.
"Yo, Jerry! Where do I park?"
"Anywhere you can in front of my house or where there are places near the houses. Those spots are first come first serve."
"Awesome, I think I'm in front of your house. I'll be right over. 2467, right?"
"Yes." My heart trembled.
I must have paced the living room over a hundred times in anxiousness. I couldn't believe I was going to see her again so soon. She knocked on the door, and I hesitated before answering it for a nanosecond. I opened it and her face illuminated my own.
"Hey! So, it's nice to see your place in the daytime seeing how the night I dropped you and your neighbor off I couldn't really see much."
"Yes, thank you for the ride that night. Please come in."
She came through the door and made herself at home.
"So? How are you? I had a few errands to run, and I was hoping we could go eat something."
"Sounds good, when are we leaving?"
"I was thinking now so that we could have more time in the day."
"Sounds good!"
We left to Zia Records, one of my favorite used record stores. It's not only because of the variety of thing the store has, but perhaps because they have a variety of incense right at the entrance with a mix of smells. My favorite mixes were vanilla, lavender and dragons blood, that amazing dragons blood. We went in just so I could pick up a CD from another of my favorite band, Linkin Park. While I searched for

my CD, even though I already knew where it was, how much it cost and the fact it was on sale, all I could think of was Sam. The stay there wasn't too long for I wanted to finish everything I could as fast as I could. Hell, I would even wait to do everything I needed to do so that I could spend time with her. But, I also didn't want to bore her if she and I were in my house for too long.

"Hey so, ready to go?" I decided to cut my errands in half or more if possible.

"Yeah! Where to next? Thanks for taking me, by the way. I've never been here before, and it's pretty cool."

When we left Zia, CD and good feelings in hand, I cut everything I would ordinarily reserve for my lonely days when I didn't have school and work. I replaced what I wanted to do with what I had to do, the errands I couldn't afford to wait on.

"I need to go and return this shirt for my mom, go to the dealership and check my car and finally go to Game Traders and pick up a game."

"Well? Let's go!"

I couldn't believe this was the girl I met one night in a perfectly buzzed state. She was beautiful, she was smart, she was funny and best of all she was interested in me. Or at least, I could only hope so.

The day continued with the stop's I needed to take and those that could wait, for her. Upon reaching my house, we had no idea of the time. It was around 7:45pm with our day completely spent, but spent together.

"Wow… I can't believe we took awhile. I'm sorry about that."

"No way! Don't even worry about it. This was the best day I've ever had in a long time. Better than the night I met you."

"You were having a bad night?"

"Well, Mimi is kind of annoying, but she's still my friend, and Stephan is weird but hey, he too is a friend. Plus you were buzzing."

"Was I being annoying?"

"Haha, kinda. But you were buzzing, and it's OK."

I can believe her. I mean, why wouldn't I? How couldn't I with her beautiful eyes and amazing smile focused on me?

"I see. Well, I'm sorry if I have acted strangely."

"It's OK yo, don't you worry."

"Well, thank you for a beautiful day today. You know you're always welcomed here."

Just as I thought this day couldn't get any better, it did.

"Hey, are you hungry? I was thinking we could order Dominos and watch a movie. Would you mind if I spent the night at your place?"

I could not comprehend what I heard. She wanted to stay with me, in my house after only a day of messaging back and forth. I wasn't expecting anything to happen, of course, but the fact remained; she wanted to spend time with ME.

"Of course you can stay!" My excitement could not be contained. How could it? It was the best day of my life.

"Sweet. I'll take the couch then."

"Oh no, I can't let you sleep on that thing. I'll sleep on the couch. You can take my bed."

I knew that she wouldn't fully accept the offer considering that she was almost like me; she was a person who gives. If I could be anyone, I would want to be like her for she was the better half of me that remained hidden for so long. At last, I could dream. And for now I could believe.

"Hmmm, well, we could do this, why don't we both sleep on the couch?"

I hadn't the slightest clue as to how to respond. It isn't every day that a beautiful girl suggests that she and I should sleep in the same space a day after meeting. Needless to say, I was new to this kind of suggestion.

"It's settled, about the pizza, what shall we get? Scratch that, I got it; one large pepperoni pizza, some wings and a one liter of Pepsi. We can order online."

"If that what will work, I'm so down."

"Excellent. It's on me tonight; you can get the next one!"

The evening was the best I had ever known. I started to realize just a little more as to what kind of person she was. She was passionate about everything she did, from living in the day to planning for the future. She helped me understand a feeling I wish I knew early in life so that I knew that this lonely road I have been on for so long had an ending. Despite my feelings, I knew I had to keep them dormant, just enough so that I could make sure that this was something I knew would last well beyond anything I have ever experienced. I kept the fate in knowing I had suffered enough.

Dawn came: I awoke only to see her fumbling in the dimly lit kitchen at 10 in the morning, and it couldn't be better. It was as if two days became one and the best part was that we could do anything we wanted for she had no work, and I had no class.

"What are you doing?" I asked, still early enough for me to catch at least one more hour of sleep.

"I didn't want to wake you, but I guess I failed."

"Naw don't worry. Did you need anything?"

She came from behind the counter and made her way towards me. I sat up and just as I made the attempt to get up, she stopped me, one arm to the chest. I still don't know to this day if she could feel my heart.

"Where ya going?"

"To open the blinds, I thought we could go out again."

She paused and then looked around. I knew she had an idea; I just didn't know how brilliant it would be.

"I am very comfy where I am. Why don't we just stay here bundled up on the couch, watch some T.V. in this nicely dim room and eat what's left of our pizza?"

Can this girl be any more amazing?

"That… Sounds like a brilliant idea. What shall we watch?" All I could think of was where this day would lead to, but I kept all focus on the here and now.

"Doesn't matter, as long as you move your ass! I want that spot you're in!" I could've given up the spot. But instead, I made her fight for it. She was strong and playful and possibly the love of my life although I wouldn't tell her that yet. It was still too soon.

We talked about our history, about what made us "us." I learned that she was a student in an accelerated college program, the kind that didn't go by semesters but rather, by weeks. She had a full-time job at a company, which her mother works for dealing with finances and hardcore executive stuff. Her mother, one of the top three employees who oversee the rest is a well-known person so naturally, Samantha's name was well known too.

"What I hate is that, because of my mom, everyone is too afraid to talk to me because they'll think I will fire them. I don't have that power."

"Really? I would assume you kind of had leverage."

"I technically do, but what kind of person would I be if I used a power that even I know is not mine to use?"

"That is fair. But I mean, even I talked to you, and I'm afraid of you.

"Oh, shut up."

I learned that she was adventurous. Her family was always the outdoor type so if I had to be stranded somewhere; I would hope it's her that I would be stranded with. The closed curtains in the living room ensured that we were incapable of telling time, like being in a perfectly lit Las Vegas casino.

"Hey, I have an idea. Hand me that notebook," she said.

"Whatcha gonna do?"

"Let's make a list, a list of where you and I are going to go, together on road trips."

I had never met a more spontaneous girl in my life; it was as if she was a living, breathing conduit of energy and happiness. I always opted out for staying all day indoors not because I always had something to do, but because the home can become a cage. All the possibilities to do something productive and instead, the majority of the time we cannot see past the couch and T.V. But this was different. Here I was, enjoying time with a girl whom I felt I was building so more than a friendship. By the time we had noticed it; it was 6:30 in the evening. The list we had created was a page long filled with various areas she had yet to visit, and I had never heard of before.

"There. This list will be just us, you and me, taking on the world."

"Sounds good. So, it's almost 7pm… were you going to spend the night again?" I had hoped for the best, but I knew I was asking too much.

"Mmm, naw. I can't stay tonight. I would but then that means I need to get up super early to go home, change, make breakfast, answer all this shit mail… and then work."

"I understand. Well, please let me know when we can hang out again. This was just amazing."

"Bueno. Will do sir. Text me, OK?"

"I will."

I walked her to the car. The skies were mimicking the way I felt. The outside air felt strange as if it was going to rain. Clouds were a dark reddish- purple color, and the sunset was casting wild depictions of shadows while the mountainsides within the outskirts of the city were slowly being approached by the thunderstorms of the monsoons. The setting was beautiful and the reflection of the beauty of the moment I was experiencing engulfed me in a euphoria I could only dream of during the countless nights spent awake in the mind of a wandering ship. We reached her car, her stuff all piled up, me with a blanket wrapped around me. I wish I could've held her then. The same way rain clouds must let go of the rain, I had to let her go. It was inevitable.

"Alrighty. I shall text you later, and we can hang out for more pizza."
"Sounds like a plan to me. Thanks again Sam. You're awesome."
"You too buddy. Later!"

We spent two whole days together just getting to know one another. It is amazing to think that with so many people on this earth, we will only meet those we are brave enough to reach. Even then, it's not a fraction of all the people on this earth. I believe I have spoken to the best one of them all.

"My heart is the bravest soul I will ever know.
He has fought valiantly by my side,
From the siege of its reality to the fall of my memory.
The wounds he sustained insured he would be granted beautiful freedom From the chains of his sadness…"

My Home. June 21st, 2013

My age might never make me wise.

Tonight was my birthday party. My actual birthday falls on the 25th of June, however, due to the summer most of those I wish could partake travel for this time of the year. I was able to send a message of my party, and if enough people showed up, I would host something. Enough people confirmed on the list and naturally my excitement was in the air considering I haven't had a legit birthday party in the longest time.

I had no concept of taking chances. For me, my past was a tattered wasteland. There was nothing I could gain from revisiting my memories. Before Samantha, I was, in a way, broken. I didn't understand what it meant to find a genuine love for those who came before proved themselves' wrong. I don't blame them entirely though. A relationship cannot work without the cooperation of both partners. The rewards are shared, but the shame varies.

My mother had mentioned I should host the party in my hometown of Nogales, just an hour away from Tucson. If I did, that would mean an entire weekend of booze, swimming, food and fun. However, that would also mean that there would be fewer people who could go and even worse, what if Samantha couldn't go?

Despite my excitement, I didn't know where I wanted my heart to be. I was at the peak of getting over my ex-girlfriend but what made it easier was the fact that she didn't deserve what I gave her. It had been about four months since we had broken up and within the first three weeks she already had her new boyfriend. I remember meeting the guy. Small, shy, afraid to speak up and ready to be her bitch. I think I speak for everyone that no matter whom you are; guy or girl, each should play their part in keeping each other happy. That being said, when your significant other lets everything and I mean EVERYTHING go, becoming the physical manifestation of the Frozen song "Let it Go", something needs to change.

Unfortunately for her, I did not accept her changes from a fit, attractive girl to an even bigger version of her big sister, emphasis on big. When trust is non-existent, and space not granted, fights on mental territory are bound to happen. Long story short; any girl I knew was a potential threat to our relationship. She hit me in the head to prove the point that she is not crazy and best of all, I'm more than confident she failed in whatever she loved, except eating.

Past remnants aside and with copious amounts of anxiousness, this night would be my one-millionth party hosted. The ice was ready, the drinks chilled. My stomach was full of a double quarter-pounder with cheese, and medium fries, a Dr. Pepper, and six nuggets all drenched in the tangy barbecue sauce McDonalds offers. I had my once good friend by my side, always the first to arrive because he was once my brother.

I had told him for weeks of the girl I met on 4th Avenue and how beautiful she was and the exhilarating fact that she would be here tonight. I wore the best attire in my closet, trying not to look like I was trying too hard to impress. The first three guests came, all eager to drink whatever variety of delectable poisons people would bring. One by one and sometimes as a group, the partygoers marched through my door. They were excited for the evening festivities to grow, happy that I could give them a place where their job and school work didn't matter for a good six hours.

As the final usual guests arrived holding a bottle or a case of beer, I rushed into my room to see my phone still charging and still lacking a message from Samantha. I knew she would make it because she said she would and it was my birthday. If she missed this night, I had ammo against her for an entire year unless she made it up to me in her way.

While I would have loved to wait for Samantha, the rest could not wait to begin pouring their shots and having them too. I knew I needed to be presentable for Samantha. While some raised their glasses and bottles, I softly wet my lips to give the impression that I was drinking. Slipping away was the tricky part; as the birthday boy AND the master of the house, I had to be in the eye of everyone. I felt that my phone had charged enough to the point that it would last the entire evening.

"Jerry where are you going?" said a partygoer, buzzed and all.

"My phone man."

"Alright well, hurry up! You need to take a shot with me!"

I entered my room and knew exactly where my phone was. It was blinking with a blue notification light. Finally, the long awaited message in the darkest shade my room has ever been was visible thanks to the bright little light.

We're on our way~ her message read. I had felt a sensation I had longed for. The butterfly effect, the kind where nothing occupies one's stomach but butterflies flying in every direction while bumping into one another trying to escape. The only knock on the door that I could hear through the noise was the last one of the evening and the most anticipated one. I rushed from my room to the door. There she was, dressed in a lovely red colored tank top, a tank top that told me she was ready to take shit from no one. Mimi was there too, someone I didn't mind but didn't care for so much.

"Hey there! Told you I'd make it."

"You did! And I am so happy that you are here. Please come in!"

I had taken the liberty of introducing her to everyone in the room since no one knew whom she was. No one had the slightest idea that I liked her, and that was exactly how I wanted to keep it.

"Everyone, this is Samantha. Samantha, this is everyone. Let the party begin!"

Everyone welcomed her with open arms, and there was no one who didn't want to meet her. It would seem that I had found a keeper. The only though that remained was how to make her mine.

"I'm glad I came. I needed this, ya know? A party, new people, a cool place to chill. Thanks."

To think I could have chosen any other location that I was familiar with, seen any number of people and possibly drank something different. To think I would have missed the one chance to meet someone I might have never met in my life. I knew I made the right choice that night, to go into Delectables, sit at the bar and move to her group when the time seemed right.

"I'm glad you said yes."

The night continued, and everyone's borders were taken down. Everyone was everyone's friend, yet all I could think about, all I wanted the night to be about was Samantha. It wasn't only a party, but a going away party for an army friend. He would be deployed for six months, all of us but his family cut off, left to wonder if he were OK. Being the new girl, Samantha was in the eye of everyone and no one would try to use his magic more than the army man himself, Travis. As a host, I had to be a floater. I couldn't just devote myself to one guest even though I'd break that chain and devote what I could to the girl I found irresistible.

Just as I wanted, she was sitting alone on the couch. Her tank top was matching the red leather couch that my mom had chosen out of a home furnishing store catalog before we had officially moved into the house. She was alone and finally, it was time to make my move.

"Hey, mind if I sit here?"

"Not at all. Great party, by the way."

"Thanks. So? Enjoying yourself and everyone here?"

She turned to face me so that we could have an uninterrupted exchange of words. Her beautiful long hair that reached her waist was in a ponytail, hanging from the right side. Her left leg crossed over her right, head askew and glasses slipping down. Her back straight and her eyes focused on me. All that was missing was her smile, and I would have melted.

"Everyone is great. You have a right group of friends."

"Why thank you, some are from work and others are friends of friends."

We must have talked for fifteen minutes. Learning small, minuscule things about her while trying to advance to the bigger picture of if she and I could become something more than just friends.

"Anyone you meet in particular that stood out?"

"Well…" She exclaimed. "Your army friend tried to use the 'I'm being deployed' card on me. It was a nice attempt, but he's not for me."

She was sharp, as sharp as you'd want anyone to be. And her beauty, the way she could level any and every defense you have to nothing more than dust and echoes… She was just that amazing.

"Yeah, he's like that. I mean, what can I say? You're beautiful."

She smiled and laughed a bit, probably brushing the compliment off as a general statement but not knowing I meant what I said.

Travis had a good friend with him, also enlisted in the army, but he was a quiet one, perhaps because he too felt that he was a fish out of water. While Travis tried his charm, his friend whose name escapes me tried his charm as well but not on Samantha. Instead, he tried charming Mimi of all people. Although he would have a lot more fun with a rock, he worked with what he had, which was either a lot or a little depending how you'd see it.

I was sure nothing and no one would ruin the time I had with Samantha. But sometimes, words can be spoken too soon, or worse, they can be thought of before being spoken.

"Sam, we have to go." Mimi said, the look of detest in her eyes.

"What's the matter?"

"Can I tell you outside, in private?"

I didn't know exactly what happened. Mimi came almost out of nowhere and looked as if she had seen a ghost. Of course, I was not about to let this ruin the evening, even though there was a high possibility of Sam leaving sooner than I wanted her too. She returned inside; Mimi still hanging out by herself in the walkway of my home, her face in disappointment, disbelief, and confusion.

"We have to go. Mimi is having some trouble."

"What happened?" The thought I had, to have to wait for what would feel like an eternity until I saw her again chilled me. I knew it would be soon, but soon wasn't enough when I had just one question to ask.

"Well… Travis's friend kisses Mimi, and she didn't want that, so she feels very wrong."

"Oh man… well if you have to go, please take care."

"I will. Sorry about this."

Samantha left with Mimi close behind. All the while, I was shaking my head for two reasons; one, why would he do such a thing and with Mimi of all people, seriously? If Carson couldn't even close a deal with himself after a night of loneliness, why would this guy go the easy route? Sometimes, people have nothing to lose. And two, he had inadvertently driven away the girl of my dreams with his stupidity.

"Dude," I still don't remember his name. "What the hell? I heard what happened."

"…"

"Fool! Go now and fetch me yet another refreshment as I am parched. From here till thy leaves my domain, thou shall be considered 'The Maiden of the retrieval of the elixir or love, life, courage and the peruse of more cordage' or as its referred to these days as 'Beer Bitch.' Go, go now fool!"

My stricter sarcasm would have been the perfect instrument to deal with his foolishness, but then I remembered that sarcasm isn't for everyone. Or perhaps it was just too damn brilliant. Personally, I decided to refrain from doing anything about it. What was done was done, and it was through no fault of my own, I just wished it didn't have to be that way.

My evening ended with a variety of mixed and drunken feelings; was I falling for Samantha? Did she even have the slightest idea of how I felt? All this and I was thinking a mile a minute. I got to know Travis's friend better whose name I finally had stuck in my head; Mike, of all army dude names and I, couldn't remember Mike. I wasn't the only one that night who had someone in mind. Mike had Mimi for some odd reason, and my once good friend had Michelle, yet another fish out of water who came to experience one of my legen-and no I will not wait for it kind sir- dary parties. Carson, although I had sworn I'd never see again was there, mostly because I knew he would provide. He also had Michelle on his mind, but thanks to his pathetic way of flirting, his attempts were seen as childish and ultimately not sexy.

"Hey girl, touch my hand. Thank you… Now I can say I've been touched by an angel." Seriously? THAT is how you pick up chicks? With the opener 'Hey, touch my hand…' No one is going to want to touch that.

As the evening came to a close it was time for the second question of the night; food, what's on the menu? We spent all the 5 minutes trying to figure out where to go for our last meal of the evening, but by this time it would be our first meal of the morning. Our choices had boiled down between Waffle House and IHOP. I didn't care considering both places had food I wanted, but Michelle wanted IHOP despite being outnumbered by Waffle House goers.

It didn't take long for me to order. My meal never changed, and the sadness towards my image never seemed to hit me where it hurt. At least, not as much as I wished it did.

With the food in belly and alcohol still surging as our bodies slowly wanted to give up, we made our trip back home. I don't know what made us want to stand outside until the sun came up, but we did. We all talked for the remainder of my birthday as the sun slowly began to burn our faces. We laughed, Travis was passed out in the truck, and the rest who joined us were also ready to call it a night. All this time and I wish Samantha were with us. She would have ordered her bowl of whipped cream, devour it and made me fall all the more for her.

I couldn't remember who went to IHOP in the end. All I remember was standing outside my house, chatting the last few minutes of morning darkness and seeing the sun rise at six something in the morning, almost seven. It would seem we moved forward onto a dawn, and I knew a specific the morning would come.

I wish I understood why we have dreams that sometimes are too real to be true. Is it a premonition or is it something else? It's definitely something. Something elusive, gnawing at our realities, convincing us there is a way to make impossibilities a reality.

My Home, July 12th 2013

We are meant to be at peace from every distance.

I have to admit; I love being social. It's a quality that my father taught me and with it comes the ability to open doors and even create a connection with others. I know that's a reason I cannot truly be alone for extended periods of time. You ever felt that sensation your home is like a prison?

That was the reason for the never-ending parties I threw. After years of failing to host when I first lived in Tucson, it would seem with this group at this location, parties were ideal for everyone, especially since my home was soundproof when the door shuts. I once again splurged on alcohol in the form of different beers and liquor just to show that no expense is too great in the company of those I loved. Plus, hosting as a B.Y.O.B. party means that people can bring their drinks and there wouldn't be anyone who wasn't enjoying the night. If people were to bring drinks, it is noted it's for everyone or it's a personal stash. That's why these parties worked so well.

I knew that Samantha was difficult to reach, but at the very least when it came to big plans she would be the first to respond. The second party she would ever attend again was another generically based party with no goal but to beat our previous tormentors at beer-pong or any other game we made up the previous party. Those I invited showed up one by one and I noticed Samantha was earlier than usual and while I questioned that fact, I quickly forgot it when I realized she was here sooner than she had ever been.

Despite all my optimism for this evening…

…There was something I couldn't shake.

There was some uneasy feeling that I couldn't understand and yet I knew it would eventually surface, like anticipating something bad at the end of a day that should have stayed productive until the very end. While the night continued with fun and laughter, I couldn't help but notice Samantha. She was less joyful and seemed to not want to be here. Before I could say anything, she had mentioned if she could go into my room. I let her have her space because it was not my place to ask if something was wrong… but I knew it was true. I could only hope she trusted me enough to let me in. When she arrived, I looked into her eyes hoping to see the eyes that, weeks ago I would look into and feel a joyful sensation of beauty and intelligence that lifted me to the heavens. These were not the same eyes I looked into. I saw a very ravaged and distraught Sam whose eyes were now sightless and gray.

I walked into my room after about fifteen minutes just to see if everything was OK.

"Samantha?"

She was doing what I wouldn't expect; crying, nearly uncontrollable sitting on the couch in perhaps one of the most powerless hunched over position I have ever seen. I was frightened. An invisible force was destroying her, the strongest girl I have ever known and I was powerless to help. I approached her, every feeling of care and support bubbling inside, but it was not the time. She looked up, her eyes were red and had been crying for reasons unknown. For the sake of her happiness, I had to involve myself in any way I could, even if she rejected my help.

"Is everything alright? You know I'm here for you."

This night I would be told a secret, a secret I swore I would never tell for she asked me not to, and a secret that even now and always must remain in obscurity.

"I know. It's just that… a memory surfaced out of nowhere."

"I'm here." I didn't know if I should have held her. But the least I could do was to sit by her side.

"I don't know if you want to hear this."

"Sam… I don't know how I can help, but if it means anything, I won't let you face these memories alone."

"Thank you… Just thank you."

She told me what happened to her; she uttered the secret I keep with me still. She trusted me enough to let me into her dark past, a past that I prayed would let her rest. Beyond the secret was what I had hoped for months, an action I waited for but an action I had preferred to do under sober circumstances. One moment we were talking and the next I found myself locked in her arms. She was the type to take charge of what she wanted and at that moment, she wanted me. She held me and took me by the back of my neck, drawing me closer to her lips. It was instantaneous.

We kissed that night. The type of kiss, you would give someone who could save you from every previous pain ever witnessed. It was the kind of kiss that would open up the pathway to a better life after the day was over or just beginning. I am still unsure that the moment we kissed she felt the same intensity I did. Perhaps it was only I, in my mind, wishing this could continue. I felt myself falling, falling down a path I had never known, the kind of path that would lead to happiness.

After a few minutes, we emerged from our cocoon of emotion and passion. I asked if she would be able to stay, but I knew the answer before I even finished the sentence.

"No, I can't. I have school very early in the morning. But I'll stay longer."

"Deal. Shall we?"

"We… should get back to your party. You are the host, after all."

She was right. I was the host, and it had been a good half hour, even more than that since I disappeared. We emerged from my room, not hand in hand but side-to-side. We stood together with mind and body synced, prepared to traverse a road a road we have traveled alone for so long together. Everyone wooed at the site of us, thinking whatever they wanted to as to what that happened in that room. I knew the truth. I immersed into the past of a girl I liked and received a kiss from her. I couldn't be happier, and while I wished it continued, I knew that I was indeed walking, hell; I was waltzing down the path of happiness.

As the night came to a close, I felt that Sam and I had that connection we wanted to have with someone. I always have the tendency to thinking ahead, sometimes too far ahead but how could I be wrong? How could this feel wrong in any way? I felt I was on the path and even after that night…

I never saw such a path.

A Cafe called "Something Sweet", August 5th, 2013

Who declares a world not green enough for its truth and all its beauties?

I must have messaged her once a day. Nothing too overbearing and nothing too blunt, I just wanted to talk. I mean where did she go? Where was our connection? Why was I left alone with the memories?

I had taken into consideration that Samantha and her busy, obscure ways, didn't have time for me after a few weeks of not getting a response. I knew with the combination of school, work, family, and other friends, she would be busy. But my thoughts didn't get too far when I remembered that we had something going for us, and now I couldn't see past that. I accepted that this would be a path I should no longer traverse, not because it was impossible, but there was no passion on her end to show me I should keep on going. But what could I do?

She held me captive in my mind without even wanting to, without even trying. Even before I thought of calling her, she called me first. Part of me wanted to answer on the first two or three rings, but part of me wanted to wait until the fifth or sixth or even, God forbid, let it go to voice mail. Anything involving her incapacitated my ability to think. After all, she was everything I could ever want, despite the waiting. I knew this must be a test.

"Hello?"

"Hey Jerry! Listen, I know I have been busy, but how about you come over with me tonight to a little cafe on Speedway called Something Sweet?"

"Yeah, sure! What time?"

"Well, head on over in the next 15 minutes. It's closer to you so you'd get there way before me if you left now."

"Done deal. See you there."

"Later!"

I had an arrangement of butterflies in my stomach, the sensation of spiders crawling up my legs, and I could feel my heartbeat in my throat for I was finally going to see her once again. I began to wonder if maybe, just maybe I succumbed to her. But even I knew, obsession is like an addiction; it only exists if you let it. The next fifteen minutes would be the most agonizing minutes I had ever know. What would I say? Would I still pretend like it was the day she spent the night at my house? This day together would be one more to add to several others that wrapped my mind in a calm sea of blissful awareness.

I arrived at the cafe without a moment's hesitation, except for a small U- turn when I missed the initial exit. I could see her Golf GT, and I saw her sitting by the window, fourth booth from the door. I walked into the cafe. It was a nice place with both booth and tables. The coffee bar served up a variety of homemade creations. The best sounding ones I couldn't pronounce. I walked up to her; her face buried in her phone.

"Hey stranger, long time no see."

"Hey! Come sit, I ordered food. Want something?"

"I might have a hot chocolate, it sounds real good."

"Awesome! Yeah, it's homemade. Everything is."

I planned to stay by her side or rather, facing her as long as I could while we were at the cafe. Even now, my mind refuses to remember what came before the words she uttered.

"… And honestly, I do that to all my friends. I just don't respond and when I do, its short responses. Don't take it the wrong way… And about us… please understand I am not in a good place right now."

"I understand."

I did not understand, even a single bit. What was it about my memory that I hate so much? Is it that I can recall everything that has ever happened to me? Is it because I can't ever forget? If I truly had to give a reason, it would be because I don't forget, and it annoys me. I am thankful for the fact I can remember the lesson that comes with the fall. If she was in this unsettling place, then I had no right to bitch about it although I would prefer a stronger answer.

She was casting away the memories of a potential "us" and I couldn't stop it. I thought of my hate that comes from my sadness and what I could do with it… everyone deals with their demons in their own way, and yet the easy way is never the answer when it comes to learning a lesson.

"It's getting late and I have to go now. I have to get up at 5 for some bullshit thing at work."

I wish I could find a way to explain this lesson. But there is no way to learn a lesson the same way. We can teach how to prepare for the end of the road, but we won't always have the same trail.

"Yeah. It's cool."

I had given up trying to fight the fact that despite the time we spent together, it was never how I wanted to spend it. I knew I was selfish but how could I not? This girl, this girl had me by my every thought and yet there was nothing she thought of me, of us.

"You OK?"

"Of course!" I never knew the empty capabilities of my happiness.

We are masters of our paranoia. We see what can happen even before it has a chance to manifest and root itself in our realities. I had nothing left with this girl. At the very least, she was honest, one of the many qualities I admired. I couldn't help but realize, as I drove the lonely drive back to my home, that she rooted into me. Our lives, whether I accepted our reality or not, would twist and tangle into my perfect web of uncertainty and madness.

As I pulled into my garage, I realized I should have never fallen for this girl. I realized I should have never entered that bar should have let Carson fight that guy who was getting into a fight with another. I would have called the taxi and gone home at 2am. Would have woken up hungover and starving, still hating how fat I was while eating a double quarter-pounder with cheese, medium fries, a Dr. Pepper and six nuggets all drenched in tangy barbecue sauce. If not for her, I could have forgotten the challenges of how sad the journey through a tattered heart truly was.

There is a gift behind every sad moment we can pull through. The gift is knowing we can pull through at all…

I let go of what I had to in order to help me defend myself from my unstoppable torment. Like the times before, I knew I would not talk to her for some time to come. Why would I want to? I have not known this feeling in a long time. If I were to gain anything out of it, it would be the lesson in the end, whenever the end of our journey decided to come.

…But sometimes, it just takes a little longer to see the end.

Who was this girl? What sort of devil is she, to have me fearing no pain and yet question who's free? It was her hour this night that could have settled this fate; freed me from that which only hindered my sake. All that would take was a kiss from her lips, reality set in as she showed me a false light.

Damned should I live in this falsehood of tears, damned if I yield while so close to the edge. I am what's' wrong and what's wrong is just me. I am no more as the last shot has missed.

There was nothing on earth that compared to the damage sustained in this hell.

Though these thoughts tore apart.
    Will it ever be seen?
        Have I suffered enough now?
            Have I done what she needs?
                And now I'm left with all my doubt,
                    I doubt the truth of my own skin.
                        My heart once stone now lies in ruins.
                            This world I create is mine to destroy.
                              Was she from heaven or my hell?
                                And did she know…
                                    That granting me the gift of life…
                                      This woman's' killed me even more.

I would reach light, but I knew. I would reach until no more. Help me stare into the void, of a world I must let go. Need escape now from this world, from a world that's left undone, no more reasons to return, and no memories to preserve.

Serenity's Birthday. September 4th, 2013

And as the tides rest, not wanting to destroy its shores further, it must to do so to cleanse what humans could not, further poisoning itself.

    I had some knowledge of what was to come, and while I had every chance to defend myself I chose not to. It had been unaccounted days or weeks since I, once again, heard nothing from Samantha.

    This day was my friend Serenity's birthday. She was to turn 22 and called to invite me to her home in the evening to celebrate. I never hear much from Serenity for the reason she is "never wrong". That means that if I don't text her it's my fault and if she didn't text me, it too was my fault. It was difficult hanging out with her, but I did the best that I could with whatever I had. I know that if I went to her place tonight it would make up for every time I hadn't texted her.

    "Jerry! Do you want to come to my place tonight for my birthday and then head on over to 4th Ave?"

    4th Avenue was a place I had not been to for a long time, not since I walked into Delectables months before, and life slowly began to change. There was almost no one for me to go to anymore considering everyone in my previous circle had disbanded months before. The group I once called my friends and co-workers turned on me through their nosiness and way of making any problem they're own for the sake of a good show. I say, fuck them. Even now, I'm glad they aren't a part of my life.

    "Yes Serenity, I will go. What time?"

    "I was thinking you should come to my place at 6:30, we can leave at 8pm to 4th."

    "Sounds good."

    "You wanna invite anyone?"

    Samantha was the first person to pop into my head. At this point, I had reconnected with old friends and even made new connections with those I had met along the way on my journey towards a healthier lifestyle. I possibly could have said no, and yet all I wanted to say Sam.

    "Yes, I do. You haven't met her, but she's awesome."

    "Is it that Samantha girl you kept talking about?"

"Yeah…"

"Sweet! If you think she's cool, I believe you."

"Thanks. See you at land-down."

"Huh?"

"Gears of War quote, playing the game now. Sorry."

"LOL."

It was a long time before her party, and I had just one call to make. I called Sam to see if she was available in the evening. She works every day of the week and just like every other weekend, I tried to invite her to anything. Half of me was ready to hear the all too familiar phrase "I want to take it easy this weekend and not spend any money." It isn't to say that Samantha is a cheap person. She makes her money, she makes her living, she pays her car, her apartment her food and everything she can because she is that independent. I can understand her want of relaxing and saving up because going out does get expensive.

I called, ready to hear the words I was all too familiar with but also, ready to hear her voice after a prolonged absence.

"Hello?"

"Hey, what's up?"

"Not much, and you?"

"Calling to see if you would be interested in going to 4th Ave tonight for a bday."

"Hell yeah! I'm down. What time?"

"Seriously?"

"Umm, yeah. You invited me."

"This is a first."

"Oh, shut the fuck up, carbon. What time?"

"6:30 is the pregame, at eight we head down to 4th."

"Cool. I'll take my car and meet you at your friends place, text me the address. I'll probably be a little late since I got to take care of a few errands, but I will be going."

"I'll hold you to that."

It truly was a first. She hadn't said 'yes' to an invite in a while, and certainly NEVER on the first try. For guys, if we ask out a girl and it's the all too familiar "naw" followed by a reason, we hope for the promise of a different date and time. We get sad but remain hopeful. We will keep it in the back of our minds that we will soon meet again, just the two of us and everything will play out how we imagine it while acting out the scenario in the shower.

If a girl asks a guy if they would like to hang out, without a second thought we say yes. Period. We will drop everything planned to see you. And even if we can't, we will try to squeeze you in our plans because all we want is to be with you.

This particular situation was different. Samantha and I had already established our feelings for each other, but we were never sure on when and if we could act upon them. Perhaps it was I fearing we couldn't be more than just friends, and my regret at not being more assertive with what I wanted to be that was my downfall. Or perhaps it was her, feeling a regret towards the thought of us that I may never understand. Whatever the case, no regret is guilt-free.

The evening had come before I knew it, and I had the sinking feeling of every possible adverse outcome that could happen. Something I learned in my time of knowing this girl was the fact that I always seem to prepare for the worst and never have any premonitions for the positive side of things. I guess I like preparing for the worst because I rather stay ready for a hard fall, fast and as painless as can be so that I may move forward faster. I continue to work on the fact that I cannot be ready for everything.

I arrived at Serenity's house just as she had asked, 6:30 in the dot. I don't like to be kept waiting and don't like to keep others waiting no matter the circumstances. Ironic how Samantha had no trouble keeping me waiting, but what could I do? I still believed. I was confused as to how we would make it to 4th Avenue considering while close to it, one had to sacrifice their privilege of drinking to ensure the safety of those who want to partake. In other words, we needed a designated driver. Like hell I was to spend money on a cab. That would have meant I get to drink less.

It was particularly windy this evening. The month of September was always a strange one here in Arizona. It was as if everyone was happy at the same time and yet you could feel the underlining sadness coming from whatever personal problems everyone had. I guess that's why the song "Wake Me Up When September Ends" by Green Day exists. Good song too.

My arsenal for the pregame consisted of a 12 pack of Miller Lite and a BevMo bag. I knew from experience of hanging out with Serenity that her friends, unless those REALLY weird ones were coming, wouldn't want beer and stick to whatever they had. I would be pre-gaming with my personal stash. As I had anticipated, no weird friends were there. It was just Serenity, her boyfriend Mark and their friend Sandy whom I dubbed 'The Sandman' JUST because her name had the word 'Sand' in it. I still think her name is one letter too long.

I knocked at the door, one hand with a case of Miller Lite, the other empty, trying to find its way into my coat pocket to shield itself from the cold. Cold does exist in Arizona. Serenity answered.

"Hey Siren."

"Jerry! You made it!"

"You expecting anything different?"

"Naw, but you having hung out or texted me in months."

"I copy and paste what you said."

"Grrr…"

"Oh relax. I brought you stuff to make you a flaming shot."

"Yaaay!"

We made our way to the kitchen. Removing my jacket and adjusting to the pleasant warmth of the house, the four of us stood around the dinner table, opening Serenity's presents and drinking. Nothing too intense since getting INCREDIBLY wasted before going out was a no-no. While everyone talked and did their thing, I prepared the shot for Serenity. It was my favorite shot to make and maybe, just maybe I could convince Samantha to try one when she got here. The shot consist of half a cup of beer, preferably a light one, recommended with Bud Light, Budweiser or Miller Lite, even though Budweiser isn't technically "light" but it should be. The shot itself is one part Amaretto liquor that tastes like hazelnut and one part Bacardi 151 and finally, some fire. There was just no way to do the performance side of the shot because we were indoors. Truth is; I wanted to do the showmanship aspect of the shot.

"But what about the fire?!"

"Drop the shot in the glass, the fire will go out and chug. Let it sit too long, and it won't mix well."

"OK, OK!"

Of course, she doesn't like beer. She doesn't like being around it or even looking at the can. You ever see anyone do the "Bwugh" face when they see a drink they despise? That was what I got from her after she took the shot.

"Bwugh… It was good, but I don't like beer."

"Sorry, but there is no other way of making it. It has to be beer." I'm sure there's another way to make the drink.

"It was good, but I'm done for now."

Anyone else?"

I ended up making the shot three more times and by that time, it was 7:40pm. Samantha had still not shown up, but I wasn't surprised. I was ready to get a call or text saying how some bullshit thing happened that blah, blah, blah and "sorry I couldn't make it" speech, but I didn't. Instead, I got a call saying she was outside and was about 30 seconds from the door. I mentioned Sam was here, and I would be getting the door myself since it was the right thing to do since she didn't know anyone.

I walked outside to greet her; the wind had still not shown signs of calming down. The wind and I shared a similar trait that evening, but like jewels shimmering in the dark, we were seen but not truly heard. She was here and after waiting for far too long; I finally saw her anew and just as beautiful as the last time. Still eating away at me with every second that passed.

"It's not the first place I would consider visiting, but she's my friend, and I owed her a visit."

"Well, that's nice of you. Andale lets get the fuck out of this cold."

We entered the kitchen, Sandy in the bathroom, Mark and Serenity in the kitchen being particularly distant. Of course, that was none of my business.

"Hey everyone, this is Sam."

The pleasantries of exchanging names and talking of what we each study commenced and I was about three beers in, not feeling any effects just yet since I didn't want the night to end too quickly. Sam mentioned of everything she had mentioned to me before on how she lives on her own, works for a huge firm, how she and I met and even some stuff of her ex-boyfriends. Nothing was unknown at this point so I wasn't too interested in her introductions since I could have told them myself if they had asked. Sam was looking particularly beautiful this evening with her hair down, her awesome black high-top boots almost reaching her knee, a teal colored long-sleeved shirt with a cute black leather vest and her purse. Dios Mio.

At this time, I had been on my diet for about two or three months. I felt like a new man, not hating how I looked and only wanting what I earned be it respect or admiration. Sam's reaction wasn't subtle at all. I guess this was why I worked so hard because if she looked amazing it would only be fair if she got what she gave in return. Because, who knows? If she saw I took care of myself, she would continue to do the same, unlike my ex who believed we were married and let herself go to the point where she looked like her older sisters stomach.

We were both leaning on the counter, drinks in our hands to start with and having a moment we haven't had in months. We could finally be alone.

"So… I don't know how to say this."

"Yes?"

"You… don't look fat anymore. In fact, you look amazing."

"Oh, so… you thought I was fat, eh?" after being 211 pounds; that was an understatement.

"I can say it now because you aren't big anymore."

"Well, thank you. I did decide to make the chance and finally take care of myself. Plus, my cardiologist said it was the best turnover I could have."

"Well, Keep it up. I like you a lot more this way."

I didn't exactly know how to take that since it wasn't a compliment, and it wasn't an insult. It canceled itself out without me trying to decide if this meant anything at all. She said what she noticed and liked what she saw. Honestly, if the connection were still there, I would have kissed her. But I couldn't. It wasn't my place and quite frankly, I needed not to open the wound when uncertainty was floating all around.

"So, pregame? Where are the shots?!" She yelled in an attempt to kick the party up a notch.

"Did someone say shots?! Don't you fuckers start without me, you hear?!" Sandy yelled from the bathroom, probably to cover up her farts.

"Yes! We will wait. Who's that in the bathroom?"

"Sandman."

"Sandman?"

"Her name is Sandy, but I call her that."

"Only you."

We decided to wait for Sandy by searching what liquor we would start drinking first. There was an abundance of liquor, but nothing that was drinkable out the bottle, they were mostly things to mix with like soda, juice and Clamato. We got lucky by finding half a bottle of Pirate Bay passion fruit rum in the back of the pantry. Apparently, I can have about five of those and not feel like I want to die. Despite Sandy's plea, we made it so she would have to catch up with us.

We poured our shots, not too eager to overfill them, but excited enough to think about it. I ended up taking a total of five shots, all over half way and all under a few minutes.

"Wow, I can't believe I can have more than I though."

"I thought you liked tequila."

"I do. But it's not to drink and then go out. It's to go out after coming back in."

"Nicely said."

Sandy eventually emerged from the bathroom, elaborate make-up on and ready for introductions. Sandy and Sam hit it off when Sam mentioned that she loves to party hard whenever she can and that this evening, it would be a party worth going all out. I didn't see the need since it wasn't THAT big of a deal, but hey, if I could get away with finding out some drunken truth from Sam as to where we stood, that's all I need.

We waited for a little longer than expected for another one of Serenity's friends. He showed up around 8:05, and right then and there I knew he would be our designated driver.

"Everyone, this is Alan. Alan, this is everyone," said Serenity after she lead him into the kitchen.

Me, Sam, Sandy and Alan packed into his car and we were off. Something was amiss since this was Serenity's party and we were essentially going to start it without her.

As we made our way to 4th Ave, Alan got pulled over for speeding. We never told him to hurry, we never said to haul ass but with his spoiler and countless amounts of useless upgrades like the annoying lawnmower-like muffler, he couldn't help but see every green light as a starting line and every other annoying as "racecar" as a potential threat to his manhood. He was lucky that the police officer was in a good mood. Doing 45 in a 25 would have you paying more than this ride was worth.

We made it to the first bar of the evening, which was Malone's, an easy- on-the-eyes place with an even easier-on-your-wallet attitude. This bar would be the first of many stops and the night wasn't too packed meaning the low prices were even lower in the attempt to bring more customers through the door. We didn't stay too long as Sandy wanted to play pool. We hopped over to O'Malley's where we spend the most of our time, at least until Serenity and Mark joined us.

It is no surprise, no surprise whatsoever that Samantha is charming and beautiful; thus, she is in everyone's eye. Some guys just stare in wonder and awe while others prepare their game to see where they would land. If Sam weren't looking at me, she would have any other guy wanting to crawl for her, even though, unwanted or not, she got just that. Of course, there was no point in thinking anything of it. She was a hard girl to impress even though she never asks for impressions. Trying to impress means you hide a piece of yourself inside, not being a whole person and attempting to create a persona that isn't there. I guess that's why she initially liked me because I didn't need to impress her. Still, it was amusing seeing others try.

I was unsure of what it meant when she got close to me. Close enough where if I had to hold her in any way, the only way I could would be with my arms wrapped around her waist. It was as if she wanted me to do just that and yet, while I love playing games, I didn't see the amusement this would bring me. While I could hold her relatively close, the aftermath wouldn't matter. Her eyes, while looking only at me were not seeing me; I didn't even know who I was looking at. I could only see her as someone who loves to play games. My attraction to her wasn't there while we were together simply because I didn't expect it at all. I don't like games when there is no destination. A journey eventually ends whether it goes left or right, up or down. It has to go somewhere.

By the 4th pool game, Mark and Serenity finally showed up late as all hell and soberer than before. I didn't think that was possible. Luckily they also drank and the night continued. Eventually, we hit the dance floor, a floor I had not visited for a long time because I simply cannot dance. It wasn't before I bumped into a tall gentleman that, remarkably, I knew.

He was a health coach who helped me get healthy with his weekly fitness classes. He ended up not wanting to work for the company he was with because as he mentioned, it was one big hustle. I don't blame him. It is a hustle, but it's a hustle that works. We parted ways, and it was the last I ever saw of him.

I managed to find the group but not before Sam pulled me away.

"Let's get a drink?"

"Lets."

We made our way to an outside bar since the amount of people on the dance floor was overrunning the already overwhelmed AC. I saw two marvelous things happen. A, some staff member was holding down some drunk kid with his face on the pavement and B, some buzzed skinny kid started hitting on Samantha. His opener was priceless.

"Hey! How are you?"

"Good, and you?"

"You look like Katniss from the Hunger Games!"

I must admit that was a good one. And come to think of it, he wasn't too far off although he probably already had more drinks than either of us. He was like a little puppy; he followed her every step she took until finally I played defense as she signaled me over and held me as if we were together. I knew exactly what was going on so, of course, I had to play the part. The reaction on his face was priceless and a little sad. He immediately said that it was a fun conversation and hoped we had a good evening. We returned inside, her face emanating with laughter after being part of a sad attempt to flirt. I feel sorry for you, Unknown Soldier.

"That was a good try."

"I did it better."

"Oh stop."

We didn't want to spend too much time at only two bars the whole evening, but we did just that. 1:30AM rolled around, and it was last call everywhere. Of course, no night was complete without a food run and what better place to go than IHOP. I started to think that perhaps I was an IHOP owner in a previous life.

The night went remarkably well. Perhaps I didn't need to know where Sam and I were, romantically speaking. It didn't matter because we could still hang out and still have fun. But there was the unwanted sensation of me hoping to be as close to her like we once were, like the night we kissed and the days we spent together. We just simply didn't have that anymore. Unless it was with others, the fun aspect of us being together was dull and fighting for something that's not there means fighting all alone.

We made our way to the cars when out of nowhere; we met up with two gentlemen that I knew I would never see again. Why was it that when I was with her we'd meet people I would never see again? They were good guys, not too drunk and still able to hold conversations. I guess it was my feelings for Sam or my hate for her disregarding everything about us that set me off when she surrounded herself with these two guys who seemed appealing to her. I never ask for much, I just want honesty.

I never got the honesty I craved out of her.

As we all walked to the cars, I could feel the silent anger inside me… brewing, unwavering, consuming and incurable. With no concern for Serenity and her birthday, for Sandy and how we never see each other, I left to the garage lot and waited for them to return. I must have paced the entire garage before realizing I was on the wrong floor.

As I searched for Alan's car, I decided to take refuge in a nearby truck and commandeer the owner's truck bed. That is why I missed my truck. It was my personal space where I could be alone and mobile.

They finally showed up, Sam still in the grips of the other two. But why make a scene? All I said was that I had a solemn phone call with my mother. No one fucks with that. We all managed to squeeze in Alan's car. Since Serenity has issues when she meets new people and doesn't have all the details revealing that person's history, we were plus two in the car. We made our way to IHOP, Samantha laying on top of the two guys and myself with Sandy in the front.

The ride to IHOP was unwanted. I would have rather made my way home, had my McDonalds and let this evening end. Once we reached our destination, I decided to stay outside for perhaps the bitter cold would shock my system and help me diminish the irrational rage inside. I must have waited outside for an hour, trying to write this all out for maybe I could transfer the hate inside for words. I searched for not only words but also any phrase, any combination of any font I could write in just to forget this all. Sam came outside at one point to check up on me perhaps ten minutes after realizing I departed for double that time.

There was nothing left to say now, and not even the truth would have mattered.

"Are you ok?"

"Yeah, I'm good. I just needed to write something."

"Why not come inside and write it?"

"I… I kinda need this cold right now. It helps the concentration."

"I like your dedication…"

"What do you mean?"

"You write exactly when you need to, exactly when you know it's the right time. That's dedication."

"Thank you. This is what I do, and I'd be damned if I silence myself."

"When you're ready, just come inside, please."

"I will."

I knew these feelings were unfounded. I mean… she was happy and free. That being said, she didn't want a serious thing, with anyone. I knew I was being selfish for thinking that she should be showing me what she feels. While I wasn't angry with the guys, the negativity I was feeling towards her was unfair. But then why toy with me? The cold honesty is 100 times better than a warm lie.

I went into the restaurant, hands colder than usual. Everyone looked so surprised to see me as if they thought I had returned from the dead.

"Hey, sit on this side!" Sam said, the two guys making room for me to cross.

"Did you finish?"

"Yeah, I got it. Thank you."

"Your hands are freezing!"

She held my hands in an attempt to warm them up. Everyone continued with conversations and me looking at the menu, unsure if I should eat something or not.

"I'll get you something."

"It's not necessary Sam, thank you though. I'm just not that hungry."

"You sure?"

"Yes."

Honestly, I wanted my usual meal at McDonalds. I was sure that those who knew me there were probably working and that I could get some sweet discounts and maybe, if I told them what transpired, they would give me free food.

We left after the last person finished their meal, and as we approached Serenity's house, I was sure that the party would continue since Sandy was here from Phoenix. She is not hard to contact but hard to find. Once again in the bitter cold, we stood debating what to do. But, before any of us received a warm welcome; Serenity had to ask herself out loud if the two new guys in the group were going to come into her house.

While her thoughts were supposed to stay in a thought bubble, we all took offense to her lack of hospitality. We decided just to let everyone go his or her separate ways. I would go McDonalds, and Sam took it upon herself to take the other two guys home. Not to hers I hoped, but that wasn't my business. Sandy said her good nights' and Mark also realizing it was a bad call on Serenity's part, apologized under his breath.

I drove home that night with a sound mind, not drunk and very much awake. I felt nothing as if I had forgotten what nothing felt like. It would take however long it had to for Sam and me to speak about "us" again. I just hoped for a better outcome. While it mattered to her or not, she knew how my mind worked. I have shown her before. I have done it countless times. We didn't speak for the longest time, this time, longer than ever anticipated or perhaps it was exactly the amount of time we needed. Either way, I have never known such peace when not constantly asking myself if she is ever going to reply.

The Buffet Bar, February 7th, 2014

Again with time and time again, we must learn the harshest lessons to teach a better life.

Time didn't exist between Samantha and me; she was always too hard to reach, and when I did, any question and any sentence would be answered by her nefarious "kk". I'm still not a fan of it. This night was my friend Lucia's birthday, and she was to turn 21. Finally, we could share a drink and tell stories in a different setting. Alcohol does well to loosen lips. I had made the decision to invite Samantha to it if only to gain clarity as to how we stood once more, just to see if it would help put an end to the animosity. Were we still friends? Was there anything left of our previous imaginations? Did staying with her and sleeping in the same bed as her make us anything? She said it was normal, but for me, it meant something. Perhaps, like many of my thoughts, they were misplaced and untrue.

- *"Hey Jerry."* read her text.
- *"Hey, what's up Lucia?"*
- *"Not much. What are you doing tonight?"*
- *"Well? Going to your bday party, of course!"*
- *"Oh sweet."*

I hadn't drunk in the longest time, not since Serenity's birthday and not in a large quantity. I knew from experience that, because of the circumstances, I would be drinking a hardy amount. And why wouldn't I? Special occasions demand an extra mile. I decided to call Lucia, to make things easier.

"Hey."
"Hey, what's up?"
"Where are we meeting again? The Buffet?"
"Yeah! Then we can migrate to World of Beer and then to 4th!"
"Sounds good, but where is The Buffet? I've never heard of it."

She gave me the directions, but they still weren't familiar. It was my guess that the place rested on intersections I've never seen on 4th Avenue before. But let's be honest, at night, you can only follow the lights and sounds and navigation is as simple as knowing which bar started it all.

"By the way, if you want to invite anyone, feel free! The more the merrier."

"Sounds good. See you tonight."

Sending a message to someone who you haven't talked in forever can be the most intense thing ever. How will they react? Will they even reply? Would they even care? With whatever amount of anxiety I had, I messaged Sam, knowing I might not get a reply. But the anticipation even after everything that had transpired, if she did answer she would come.

-Hey. How have you been Sam? Listen, tonight is a friend 21st bday party. She invited me and said I could bring someone along, and I want you to come with me. It's been a long time, and I just want to see you, you know? Let me know what you think and if you can.

I wasn't sure she would answer in a timely fashion. She's not known to respond at all. Even without a quick answer I readied for my day and prepared for the night. The fact she replied at all was a miracle.

-Hey, I got your message. Yes, I want to go! It has been forever! I don't plan to stay anywhere, and I can't drink a lot because I have a few things I need to take care of. But we will defiantly have a few beers, maybe a shot and I'll drive us. I'll let you know when I am outside your house.

When I read that message, I could feel a strange sensation overcome me. I must admit that the mixed feelings of knowing I'd see her and knowing that it will be all I can manage to gain drained me. I would see the girl I cared for but couldn't do anything but watch, wait, as I would be left alone to care for her.

The night approached and was getting dress tips from my mother. "Wear this better shirt I got you!" and "You wear that all the time!" were all I could hear. Nothing was good enough yet I looked good in anything; this, of course, was from my mother. My father was in the living room probably thinking the same thing; I should just go naked if nothing is good enough. I received a message I haven't seen in a long time.

-*"Hey! I'm outside your place."* Read her message.

-*"Hey, I'm just about ready. Come on in. You'll finally get to meet my parents."* I replied, one arm out of my sleeve and my pants falling from the lack of a fastened belt.

I told my parents about this girl and everything she made me feel. They were eager to meet her because I made her sound like a saint. They didn't realize what kind of hell she actually put me through. I had hoped to an end of that hell after tonight. She knocked at the door while I mentioned that it was for me, and if someone could let her in, that would be great. Samantha came in, as I was still getting ready.

"Sam, I'll be right out!" I shouted, still trying to look as good as I could for the girl I worked so hard with to create a connection. I came out several seconds later, and I saw her; her beautiful long hair, her always-enchanting body and with the smile I had not missed in months.

"Let me introduce you, this is my mother, Fernanda. And over there on the couch is my dad. Can you guess his name?"

My mother and father both stood up ready and excited to meet her. My dad has this ability to let out the best dad jokes ever heard. I knew he wouldn't miss this opportunity.

"Hello Samantha. I am Gerardo's father, Gerardo. As you can see, I named him with a manly name." Thanks, dad.

He said his hellos before returning to the couch ready and eager to meet the second person of the evening, the game. It didn't matter which game it was. My mother was also standing and as always, she does the hug-lean in- kiss on cheek thing.

"My name is Fernanda. Please to meet you, finally." My mom said in her best English.

"Same to you. Jerry tells me you guys are awesome."

"The Best!" Replied my father.

After about ten more minutes of trying to figure out the best hairstyle, my mother and Sam talking to one another. It was interesting to see them getting acquainted so fast. She has that ability, and if the girl I like is beautiful AND can speak Spanish, my mother instantly approves. Finally, it was time to head out and enjoy the venture that was to come. We headed out to Sam's car. The poor little Golf GT was still standing. I could almost feel its pain.

"Eyy, saves a donde vamos?"

"Simon. The Buffet. Never been but its close to 4th."

We reached our destination after a few U-turns and a lot of aggressive driving. I have to say, Sam cussing in Spanish is very attractive. "Hijo de Tu Madre" and "Que chingados?!" and my favorite, "Mira wei, to voy a hechar una buen putisa" were all just so romantic. I'd be lying if I didn't say how curious this aggression would be under a different circumstance.

I had thought, even before the evening began that I was a bit tired of this endless yo-yo lifestyle of ours. One night we are as if we never drifted and then like a plague, we didn't see nor talk to each other for however long we each determined, usually a one-sided thing.

We drove for what seemed forever, as neither of us knew where this place was, and our GPS was being less than useful. At last we found the place; it looked straight out of a movie and for all it intended to do, it had a unique way of presenting itself. It had a floodlight shining on the door. An elaborate hallway style decoration scheme with decorative pots and plants and a small railing and it had what I believed was grass legitimately growing on the dirt portion of the sidewalk. It was defiantly different, and you could hear the cheers coming from inside.

We parked a safe distance from the establishment, and sat in the car just for a bit, preparing ourselves for the cold that awaited us. All the while I wanted nothing more than to ask her what my heart was screaming me to ask. But I couldn't. I knew from the previous encounters that she just didn't want anything to do with a relationship, even though she had shown me what a perfect creature she was. Even though, I'd do the impossible for her, whatever impossible meant.

I sent Lucia a message that we had found the place. I had an overwhelming fear that something was not right. I didn't feel like a fish out of water, but I did feel a type of disconnection. Lucia was with her band mates who together formed the group Diluvio AZ, and while I knew two of them and had met the others during their first show, I didn't know them enough to feel welcomed. But, alcohol was around so I would know them all entirely by the end of the night.

We were finally off the car, and as we made our way inside we had a proper greeting. "I have missed you!" I took that to heart and yet I didn't feel that sting of it when I realized I meant it more than her. I took that to every corner of my being and yet it didn't mean what I wished it would mean. I am unsure if my parents saw the manifestation of the sting. Something, however, was simply amiss. While excited for the celebration she also seemed disheveled; her smile was worn crooked, and her eyes had lost their gleam just like that night, long ago. "I missed you too, Sam."

We didn't stay long at The Buffet, and I was more than excited to begin the barhopping. I had the perfect play; we traverse to World Of Beer then jump to O'Malley's. We cross to Malone's with the final destination being Delectables.

I did not expect to return to the bar where everything started.

We made and unexpected stop at Mr. Head's and bumped into an old friend named Jesus Camacho A.K.A, Taco. We exchanged the usual bro hug followed by what were we doing with our lives. He had graduated and gave me a verbal invitation to a party he was planning. I had accepted and promised to make it when the date came.

"Y ella? Quien es?"

"La Samantha."

"Novia?"

"Desafortunadament, no. Pero es una buen amiga."

"Ua. If there is a chance wei, take it. She's beautiful."

"I'll keep that under advisement, haha. Have a good one."

We departed and our night continued. Samantha had finally loosened up, and she was so relaxed her generosity showed. She bought the 9 of us a round of a lemon drop shot, salted at the rim mixed with Gray Goose vodka and lemon schnapps, the good stuff. We all mingled and chatted, told embarrassing stories as people asked if Sam and I were a couple, and if not, we defiantly feed off each other's energy. It would seem even those who barely knew us thought the same as me. But I digressed.

After the shots had worked their way into our systems, everyone went back to talking amongst themselves. We saw who was too much of a weenie to take the shot without making a face. I took the chance and leaned towards Samantha.

"Having fun?"

"Yeah. I'm glad you brought me."

As the evening continued with drinks and laughter and the various barhopping I remembered why I couldn't hate Samantha, even though in my time alive I made a vow. Anyone who would ever hurt me in this manner would be cast aside in my mind, never to cross me again. Any and everything we shared would be forgotten, written away in my pages and sealed within to hold the pain of that encounter and thus never forgetting what it means to get hurt.

I honestly believe hate doesn't become apparent until someone crosses you. I do believe in the fact that once you have been hurt, you learn what it means to hate. All I could think from the moment Sam threw me into this wasteland was how I could let her into my world to experience this hate of mine... But I could never bring myself to do it. It was me who wanted solely to be with her. I let my selfishness consume me.

We finally reached our last destination, the place where Sam and I first met. Where nothing became apparent until our time spent together and various texts and chances to meet turned from anticipation into a suffocating anxiousness.

"Well everyone, this is the place."

Just before we reached Delectables Lucia was happily drunk, her friend Claudia had apparently no knowledge that alcohol was alcoholic and was passing out, and the rest of the group was swimming in their minds. We received various "ooh's" and "Ahh's". We made our way inside, and as the rest of the group was gearing up, having their time, I reserved us a table outside. Sam was the first who saw me; she did something that was the cause of all my defenses failing again; she kissed me on the cheek. Once again, I was lost. Once again, I had to compose myself and not let a simple gesture turn into something that wasn't there, something that wasn't meant to exist. It was my feelings for her.

Despite being where it all began, where I slowly descended into madness, I was at peace. The night had gone smoothly and with nothing that pointed me towards my felling's for Samantha and as I shook off he gesture, I remembered just how far this journey had taken me. While there were mini instances where I allowed myself to think of her, they were not enough to act upon for I finally found a balance between what we were and how I wanted us to be.

As we made our way to the bar, Sam was a bit closer to me than usual. She never did that and would never give me the hint considering our silent and apparently unnoticed agreements. I must admit, I was a little buzzed from the evening and wasn't ready to stop. The weight I had lost in the months before had lowered my tolerance for the sweet venom. But at the very least I could drink less and spend less for the desired effect.

Without even realizing it, Taco was right next to me and with a particular shove, the same shove her gave me at Mr. Head's, I knew who it was.

"I see you're following me!"

"No way, Taco. You seem to be developing my taste in establishments."

We laughed it off and offered one another a drink. He wouldn't have me paying for one and I were not about to skip on a free drink. Of course, I needed to repay the favor.

"What's your poison, Taco?"

"Fireball shot. You can't let me do it myself."

"Hmh… Let's go."

We took our shots and Sam was still very close to me, enjoying the faces I made. I'm not and have never been too fond of Fireball shots. Realizing the discomfort I was experiencing she ordered me a Dr. Pepper.

"Hey, here. Drink up. Chase it away."

"Ooohhh, Dr. Pepper, sweet. Thank you, Sam."

"By the way, here's your recipe for what you got your friend. It was twelve bucks with a three-dollar tip. I wrote out the total for you so that you won't forget. Please place this in your pocket."

I didn't know what to think of what was happening. She was not being herself, and I didn't want this feeling to go longer than it should. She was a good friend, but a girlfriend she could never be.

"Hey everyone," said Lucia "let's sit outside!" The table I had reserved was finally cleaned off.

The weather was relatively cold for Tucson, a prize that every Tucsonian loves because bundling ourselves up is something which can only happen in one of the two seasons Arizona has. I had one of my favorite hoodies on so of course I jumped at the idea of wearing my hood. We were still missing some from our group, and I took it upon myself to prepare the table.

"Sam, you coming?"

"I'm going to the bathroom then for a drink. I'll meet you with the rest."

"Done deal."

The table I asked for was big enough for all of us. It didn't take long for me to spot others from our group. The only other one from the band that I knew was Eddi. He was a good friend and wanted to repay me for the generosity Sam showed. He got me a beer and helped me round up the others so I wouldn't be alone. Just after Eddi left to find the rest Sam came from the opposite door into the patio and began scanning for me. She found me after I waved my arms, cell phone in hand.

"Hey, I got you a beer."

"Oh, awesome. Eddi got me one too. He wants to repay you for the shot."

"Well, I'll ask for something a bit later."

"Eddi went to find the others."

"Yeah, I am a bit concerned about your other friend, Claudia."

"Yeah, she's passing out and had way too much. It's OK. Eddi is taking care of her. No harm will come to her."

"Awesome. I'll go to the bar and get them.

Whether by fate or misfortune she had kissed me. The slow, invigorating venom of yesteryear finally seeped within every vein in my body despite my attempt at keeping them at bay. I was cursed, locked alongside a passed wretched life where nothing went right once again. I fought each feeling that surfaced, but I could not stop my heart. I had no right to. The pain of not trying was worse than being able to see my feelings and never acknowledging them. I was happy again for the first time in a long time… but sometimes the darkest version of ourselves lie within our most joyfully memories and most joyful of moments. I knew nothing good would come of this, but I traded a few moments of happiness I had longed for with this girl for the next few years of never talking to her again.

I couldn't remember the conversations around me. All I could hear was my own heart beating, uncontrollably and yet still in rhythm as my thoughts agitated my being, giving me the sensation of lightheadedness and the emptiness of floating within the dreamscape. I found peace.

Words remained unspoken as if anything said would ruin the moment. All I could do, the only euphoria I could feel was the feeling of her soft lips on my cheek. Her arms so perfectly wrapped around me, my eyes trying to lock with hers as the memory of a time before came rushing back. She didn't say a word except sit close to me. She couldn't stop smiling, and I couldn't stop thinking about what this all meant. Finally, something was happening. But the happiness is only skin-deep.

The evening drew to a close, and we decided on getting a slice of pizza across the street. Finally, we didn't go to IHOP. We were all without food and the alcohol was becoming more volatile. I noticed that Lucia was not of sound mind and chose to stay out of the line, crying on the side as if she had done something beyond comprehension. We walked back to The Buffet; everyone lost in his or her state of mind. Everyone from that night managed to cram in a taxi while I and Sam drove to my place…

What leads you down a very darkened path of a world that you tried so hard to create? What was the bridge that was once a monument to all the personal sacrifices, whatever they may be for whatever reason and where was it now? Who took it down and with what tools? Only the builders know, but we can never accept that they were the ones who tore it all down.

The ride home proved the most difficult. Alcohol aside, I spoke every word as it were my last. Truth is brought out with alcohol, even if it must remain silent. I learned what it meant to be shown I was worth something. I earned what it meant to hate. Our paths crossed and I was more than ready to become whatever she wanted out of someone. I was comfortable letting down every last defense leading to my otherwise tattered heart, fractured and bruised from the countless toils of a dream gone mad.

"I don't want you to have to wait for me."

I can't ever understand this utterance. Throughout our time, she had mentioned this over and over and again until I had a connection to make. Was I was not worth it? Did she not want a stupid person like me to wait for someone so incredible? Could she not bring it upon herself to destroy me completely? Or was it true? Was it true she didn't want me to have to deal with whatever problems she had? Was it indeed unfair of her to keep me waiting, even though that is among one of many hardships? I've yet to be given clarity.

I cried in her car as she watched, not saying a word, probably witnessing exactly why she didn't want to be with me. My honesty had become my weakness. I had contemplated many times before if I should just become an asshole like every other guy. I thought of how easy it would be to get whomever I wanted, to be however I pleased, adding to a growing list of assholes… But I couldn't bring myself to break what my father taught me.

"Be the person you believe you should be to shape your world and add to the beauty of the overall existence of humanity." My father would say.

The final gesture I made to Samantha was grabbing her hand and with her long nail from her index finger I slashed my forearm from the top of my arm to the bottom of my wrist… Symbolizing she had finally killed me. That she had succeeded in destroying whatever else I held dear between us. I had never known a deeper pain than what she had accomplished, it seemed I could never have someone so beautiful in every aspect of my life. That night, the circuits of the imagination connected alongside my tattered heart. If I were to be in this putrid state of mind, I should remember what I felt throughout so that I may never forget again.

I couldn't remember if I looked back when I staggered across the street from where Sam parked her car. I couldn't remember if I said anything before I hear her car speeding away at an unknown speed, perhaps wishing she could run away from the memory of my disheveled performance. Steps felt like miles; straight lines became curved, unbalanced and sitting down became freefalling. All this and I hadn't even made it to the door.

One key became many, noises became amplified, and the humming of the refrigerator became soothing. The green glow of the stove's clock light, as well as the microwaves light, helped me see the outline of the four stools and the countertop of the kitchen. The ice falling into the ice dispenser created intriguing and unique sounds as they fell into the ice tray. I was drunk, but not incapable of creating.

The small amount of moonlight coming through the doorway was just as bright as daylight, but it couldn't reach too far. It only made it a few feet into the home while barely touching the corner of the couch and was nowhere near strong enough to make the dining area visible. This day was finally over. At least, I needed it to be.

In the moment of totality and with the balance of an infinite sadness towards an indifferent end, I was not too powerless to create. I knew that this night had changed me, and even though I couldn't care about anything else except sleep, I knew I had to make sure I'd never forget.

With sadness, I could not understand.
With anger, I could not see.
With joy, I could not act.
With disgust I looked at myself.
With fear, I could only imagine.

Who was I to wish such a reality upon myself? In what way was I in any position to ask for understanding?

My words needed the ears of my tormentor any yet it is easy to ignore a call. But in this day and age, you cannot unread a text message.

A poem about you will be written.

A poem about you will be drawn.

Whether the lives of an individual clan is created of within our spectrum of knowledge is gone; I love you. No one, nothing is seen as a forgotten dream. I place myself with the undivided. I see myself with the undigested.

To see again what I am not worthy of.

I dress myself in the tears of what's forgotten to understand the tears what's left to understand. What pain dilutes the water, away from shaky hands? I see what calm dark water of yesteryear where I held commands. Drawn, bleeding, tired and still hoping for the love of your calm dry hand.

Off the record

When you see this in the midst of every message you have received

…

Nothing would have changed.

I know I'm not worthy. I know you think of nothing else but how you can calm me down into a corner and say you're not enough; to say you're a part of an ever-expanding consciousness

…

Stretching the fabric of whatever it was I believed in. I cannot live without you and yet I have to. Despite you looking after me. Despite you actually caring. Despite every other person who convinced you that you are shit

...

I was there. The hardest part is you tell me not to care. Where does the mind feel numb and where does the heavy heart grow cold?

It happened consistently; when you were told you were useless and I was told you were hungry.

-J-

It's the last time I'll ever have to know you again.

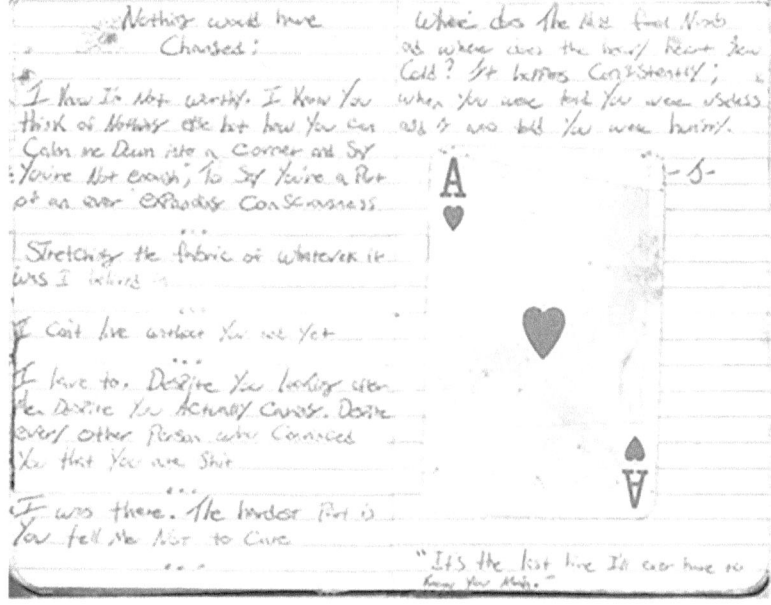

I tossed my phone on the couch after wrestling with the perfect words to describe my thoughts. I could not write these words in my journal at that moment for the words I needed to use couldn't be directed from my mind to my hand.

I didn't know if she would read this and respond. I didn't know if she would even care. What would our future hold after tonight? What was left to know of me after everything I held dear was known? Only after tonight could I reread that message on my own, sober and alert before I could make it a permanent addition to my history of lessons.

It's amazing to think that every single word we need to express ourselves resides within the confines of our mind. But most of the time we are too afraid to use them; we are afraid of creation for we fear we may never be as creative again. In the darkest moments, our hearts can shine like a beacon of hope, illuminating our otherwise darkened view of the world. We must fight to understand what we can prevail through.

Bisbee. Sunday March 2nd, 2014

The sun has now shutdown, its last light now fading. Slowly, calmly, even light can slip into the darkness.

Was it months before I could remember? In my head it was. It was just as long as I needed and then the memory of my performance came back. It replayed over and again, the morning like a permanent dark over my eyes, hours stretching and pulling with no end in sight. Essentially I was hung- over. But that was the day after, and now it had been a few weeks since then.

I woke up just like every other day; wondering how and why I let myself become consumed by the thought of her while trying to piece together the strings that were cut. I hoped there would be a way to mend them anew. Some pieces were too perfectly cut in half to the point where, although their other half was a perfect match, the dangers of reconnecting them were too high. I feared I would feel the pain still surging through each one, burning and boiling within hoping to reach my heart again.

There was nothing particular about today. My parents came for the weekend; school was just that, and I had nothing to do until I made the effort. But through it all, I did not expect to wake to a message from her. I had already made up my mind never to speak to her again. It was perhaps curiosity or maybe it was I wanting to know what she could want, considering she never sends a message first. For whatever reason, I replied.

-What are you up to? Read the message.

I couldn't believe she was curious about me, wondering if I was to make anything out of today. I didn't know if I wanted to risk reopening such fresh wounds, and I didn't know if my performance of that night was still a valid reason for her to think anything of me. Something inside told me to be honest. Like the honesty I had shown her previous times, it would be fitting for I to continue down my path towards a better person.

-Nothing. Why? What's up?
-I want to go to Bisbee today... Wanna come with?

I remembered from the list we wrote together the night she came to my house and stayed with me for an entire evening, back when we first met. Going to Bisbee wasn't on that list, but why not have a late entry? I asked who else was going. All she had planned for that day was for her and me to go together, alone and enjoy the trip and create a memory. Wish copious amounts of hesitation a replied with a yes. I had forsaken everything I had ever known. Those who bury themselves in my heart and then decide to unearth themselves, taking a piece of my heart with them, allowing only the sorrow of their absence to fill the void.

For one reason and one reason only I let myself think of her. I had finally understood that it was my fault, but I also understood that I am no one compared to her. I loved her, and yet I could never be with her. To be her friend was far too difficult. Even now, her image haunts me in my sleep. Everything about her was where it should be, like God taking his time, creating the most beautiful girl I might ever know again and creating her with such a determination and an unwavering lifestyle. But what could I do? My heart, although happy, was also being hurt. Half of me couldn't believe she still wanted to talk to me and yet the feeling of not being wanted drowned me. If I wanted her in my life, she could only be a friend. This trip would test my fortitude.

I drove to her house, a drive not taken in months, perhaps even for a year. I remembered the turns, remembered the distance… remembered how she answers the door; opens it, runs to her room, runs in the kitchen and then gives a jump hug with a beautiful smile, an unmistakable laugh and is dressed so cute. What little time she does have is the opportunity to make a difference, experience something new, creating beauty from nothing. I've never met a more determined person.

"I have missed you!" I still took those words to heart and could still felt their all too familiar sweet sting. I would still feel my heart, happy and living while knowing it will not be heard. "I've missed you too, Sam."

We packed her car. She loved to drive, and I was low on gas but wouldn't mind filling up the Jeep.

"Hey so, you'll get the next trip, right?"

"Of course, Sam." I wondered where we would go next.

The trip commenced and everything I was afraid of vanished. I feared I would slowly recall the events that had transpired. The thoughts of yesteryear gnawing at my heart, helping me feel the euphoria I could only feel in my dreams. But it didn't happen. In my realization of all my mistakes, in the thoughts of a dream that cannot manifest into a reality I learned why I wanted to keep Samantha in my life.

"I'm very happy you decided to come with me… I knew you would be the one who would say yes. I had thought of others, but you were the first I texted. I knew if you said no you would have a excellent reason for saying no."

I thanked her. Something in her mind was sharp enough to think in that way regardless of my most recent performance. I wanted to keep Samantha in my life for the reason she would be real with me. It was difficult shaking the feelings, but I knew they had no chance of living within my heart any longer. Those same feelings had died in her heart long ago, or they simply didn't have what it took to exist. I didn't feel the emotion. I didn't feel the euphoria that once lifted me to the heavens. All I felt was the stiff breeze that comes from opening a window on the highway fresh air and sunlight.

The road was winding and quiet. Not a car in sight except for the usual trailer or semi-truck making its way up north. There were no clouds in sight and to my knowledge, there wasn't a damn think I knew that was in Bisbee that I wanted to see. But it wasn't the case. I was with Sam; we were on a road trip, and things were finally moving in a direction she and I could agree upon.

We talked for the duration of the journey, not mentioning anything about us and instead focusing on what might be the next step in our lives. She was passionate about her mother opening a new finance firm and would have a secure job. Me, I was to go to L.A in June for an internship with Dream Careers. We reached our destination at around 1:30pm. The climate had changed; there was an unnatural cloud formation, and while the weather reports didn't indicate rain, it did indicate thick clouds by 4Pm, possibly thunder. Oh, what a beautiful and destructive element thunder can be. Tis' the purest form of fire.

We decided to have lunch in an underground hotel/restaurant called Café Cornucopia. Once again, she ordered her favorite desert after her meal. If the memories could do more than remind me of a happiness of back then, I would have appreciated it. There was more we could do and our main goal besides fraternizing with the locals about historical facts and hobbies, we wanted to visit the rainbow staircase that gives a magnificent view of the city. I must admit, Samantha knew how to dress well. It was a shame I could never tell her what she meant to me within the grand spectrum of my reality, but at this point, it was irrelevant. She meant something to me in an entirely different way now, and the actions I was displaying now were proof of that.

I still search for the girl of a lifetimes wish.

Once we reached the summit of the staircase and saw the city and its beauty. Once the fresh air filled our lungs, our breath was caught, and souls soothed, we decided to make our way back. We stopped at a candle shop we noticed on the way up. The wind was picking up and having our jackets didn't seem like such a bad idea now, not since a few hours earlier the sun was shining bright and the all too familiar dry heat was abundant.

We reached the shop, eager to get warmed up. She hugged me by the doorway as the door closed behind us.

"Hey, thanks again. I wanted to do this for a very long time."

"I'm thankful you thought of me. I'll add this to the list just to cross it off." "Do you still have it?"

"Of course I do. And your email as well, I never emailed you the list… haha."

"Well, you be sure that, when you can, to get that to me. I want to see what else I wrote."

"Deal."

We walked around the shop for a good while looking at the various and intricate candle designs that were all made by hand. The woman who made the candles wasn't as talkative as we hoped, but she still welcomed us warmly, hoping to make a sale. The sun had fallen fast, but that was because mountains were blocking it. Oh, if they could speak. The stories they could tell and they history they have seen. Our trip came to a close, and the rain we heard wouldn't reach us came, pleasant and cooling against our hot skin.

Aside from various pit stops, the drive back to my home was the most peaceful one I have ever had while driving to or from her place. Nothing, not even the slightest thorn of a memory pierced my thoughts. I had finally learned the peace of co-existing with what I wanted and what needed to be. To think I would lose her in the most ridiculous way possible, through the actions of one who has yet to outgrow acting childish. Samantha taught me that there would always be casualties in the theater of love, for love and war are synonymous. But war is natural, the invention of a threadbare heart longing to feel anew, But…

She has an art for disappearing.

Weeks passed after out trip, after an attempt of reconnecting, after what I believed was a step in a new direction. I hadn't heard from Samantha since then. Perhaps it was for the best or perhaps it was crunch time in school. She was a trooper with her accelerated six-week course classes. It wasn't that I expected a text or a call anytime soon, but I had always hoped so. I considered myself as her period; I came out only once a month and not even for the recommended amount of time then like the scare factor of being pregnant, I come back.

I despise having to check up on people who wouldn't do the same for me. It's just my thing. If I care for you, I'll show. All I ask for is equality It was not because the need to see if she was up to anything that caused me to open my Facebook, but rather because it was a slow day. Just before I was to do homework I'd do my morning ritual of checking to see if anyone gave a fuck about anything I posted. It's a feel-good thing. But I digress.

I received a notification that she had sent me a message through a Facebook app. The message read that she had a new phone and couldn't contact me, that I should send her a message so she could have my number once more. I didn't want to text her. Her not having my number was my chance to not only stay under the radar but also never have to be found again, unless she came to my house. I learned to co-exist with my flaws, not hers. Despite me thinking she was perfect she was perfect in my heart, but my mind and all its investigative powers saw it fit to find mistakes If only to help me clarify my surroundings. Again, for whatever reason I decided to answer…

"Hey, here's my number. Notification told me to message you. Here ya go!"

I should have known… It didn't matter if I did or didn't text her that day for she wouldn't answer for an undetermined amount of time. She just wanted my number to not use it. At this point, I have reached my indifferent end, with her and with whatever our friendship represents.

It mattered not, for I have always been one step ahead of her.

I remembered my most recent endeavor when she asked for my number. I remembered that "recent" is irrational. There is only here and now and right here, right now, this all happened a long time ago.

My Home. May 29th, 2014

To make a change, there needs to exist the chance to make it.

It had been weeks since our last encounter. I knew deep in my mind there was no reason at all to feel any emotional pain I once had. Part of me believed we moved passed all of our encounters and yet, part of me knew there was still something lying in the shadows of my mind that I could not fight. Luckily, it was exactly what I expected. The light I once shared in her eyes was finally receding into the shadows from which it resided.

Whether by fate or misfortune, she called me. Her call lightened my day, but only as much as I considered her a friend. A friend is not one who only seeks you out when something will benefit them. The feeling that she finally saw me as someone who she can talk to about whatever was necessary was remarkably interesting, or so I thought. But the call was not what I wanted and yet it was exactly as she said. She called in hopes I would help her move to a new apartment. I must admit, perhaps it is my undoing in life to try to help those I care for that I can sometimes never say no. Or perhaps, the most likely fact, she was secretly or unknowingly exploiting my kindness. Either way, I said yes because she was a still a friend.

"Hey! Can you do me a favor?" "Of course, Sup?"

"Can you help me move things to my mom and dads house? I'll pay you in gas or food. Yeah?"

To be honest, I was happy to help. In a way, it's what I do. I cannot help but be myself and do good; the reward posted by her would just be a way of saying 'thank you.'

I didn't have much to do during the day so the activity of lifting, packing and driving didn't sound too bad. This would be an interesting mini road trip to her place. I had no idea this 'mini' road trip would take me to an area of Tucson I've never known and without her help, I'll never see again.

The drive to her home was just as long as I remembered. Who knew I would always pass the mini cafe Something Sweet, where she told me, in code, she just wanted me as a friend months before. Who knew

I would still be driving this wondering road after a year of constantly fighting back and forth with everything that has transpired, who knew I could not give any more fucks.

    I reached her place, three cars being packed with mine being the awaited fourth car. I got to meet two of her friends and an uncle of hers and deep down I knew I would never see them again. There had to of been a pattern somewhere. Sam was walking to her place from an enormous truck getting whatever she could. She dressed in her formal work clothes indicating that she had just got off work. It's amazing that, behind that uniform, she could transform into a beauty beyond comprehension. But, I had no time for that. All that remained was helping her for perhaps the last time.

    Moving the items she needed wasn't why I wanted to help. It was driving to a place I've never been before that made me want to help. I knew she would live in an area of Tucson where it would encompass the most beautiful areas to see the sunset and sunrise.

    Nothing was mentioned after everything was done. I met her parents, I met her friends, and I got to eat for free at Buffalo Wild Wings. All this and I just wanted to go home. There was no hold on my soul anymore. My mind was not wrapped in an endless imagination. My care for "us" was no more.

An Unknown time, Months and Months later...

What does it mean to be a friend? Is it a set code of conduct, unspoken but learned through interaction that causes us to care and want to continue to be part of an individuals life? I have never known such a truce behind a relationship when it ends and yet, I need not know. Samantha and I never had a relationship. There was never the opportunity. Over time, I learned my heart was merely confused as it has been for so long, continually broken only to be rebuilt and find a better, more perfect form. Perfection is a state of perspective; No one is perfect, and our eyes define perfection through mere want and selfishness. We seek to find someone better than ourselves, regardless of the lens that covers our eyes.

Samantha had been the better part of me for reasons unknown. She was beautiful and perfect, but my vision blurred. A person like that cannot exist and yet, for a brief moment that was my reality. I stood side by side with her only to remember that the threshold of fantasy borders with unyielding reality. No one would understand what my sorrow meant. No one can learn the lessons in the same way as me; lessons that are necessary to live and yet, the feelings are all the same.

I can safely say I lost a part of myself when I met her, first in the spectrum of a form of love I have never known and then through the darkened dungeons of my hope. I was systematically shut down, like an old defeated man trying to stay long enough to make a difference. But now I realized it wasn't just five days. It wasn't even eight; it was a lifetime's worth of being shut down, slowly and without the chance to thread the unknown in time.

I know now what keeps me wanting to see her again, I understand why somewhere in my heart I decided she would be staying. I can remember everything that came before us and not flinch at the idea. I was ready to give whatever I had to for this girl, knowing no one else would come after. But that was my heart's lie. My heart doesn't know anything beyond its pleasure but at the moment of pain, it cannot stand the thought of one happy memory that comes from the thought of her, whoever she may be.

We can bend and break by anyone's will, we can become stronger than we ever imagined. We can recall what has happened, when it happened, how and why if only to remember why the memories still exist in the present after swearing the memories would never come back.

Where I must not hold on, I cannot let go. The friendship that was tested and strained for what seemed like an eternity finally had a solid foundation. It was proof that we have been rooted in the others life forever, but sometimes there is no telling how long forever lasts.

My Home, February 5th, 2015

Built with a heart, broken by un-started love… so slow.

    The heart is a veteran of the trade that is a coincidence or perhaps the unfortunate victim of that which we call fate. Fate is an unyielding secondary force of pure chance that decided the course of life long, long ago well before the first idea of an infinite 'I am I'. The heart and faith are two sides of the same coin. Fate is a beautiful thing. We hope for the best without wanting the worst. Me, I always think of the worst first chance I get. It helps deal with the reality of it all. I say if you must cry, cry in the past. It can't get you there.

    Falling means something, and if that fall breaks us, we might break into something beautiful.

    We fought like hell… we fought through it. But we never made it out. Wounds were sustained, and yet nothing kicks you into reality like a cold sweat. What did it all mean? At what point to we become so devoted to our dreams that they scare us? Despite the question of what it meant, I knew exactly what it was. I just like tricking myself into thinking I'm not that smart. I hadn't talked to her in a long time, not since my graduation from the University of Arizona in December. What a strange time to graduate; the last school year is up, it's almost Christmas and the New Year is just around the corner. Perfect timing. But it wasn't for selfish reasons that I hadn't talked to her. It was all way too natural at this point.

    2:46:01 in the morning isn't that bad a time to wake up. Trying to fall back asleep is usually a coin toss; maybe I'll sleep, maybe I won't. It usually depends if there is something on my mind worth divulging into. I was falling for her again and why shouldn't I? Recollecting our history and the times we managed to see each other again made me realize we are the best couple if only we were a couple. But, I was committed at the time, and she was nothing more than a friend.

    I guess I allowed myself to become reacquainted with the feelings that dragged me through hell and back because I was remembering what it was like being single. I don't like being able to recall all the happy memories of my exes for dragging along are the clouds that eventually found their way into my vision of memories. But she and I, we were never together and what happy memories I have cannot be hated as such.

I remembered of January 29th, 2015. That single call still angers me. "I think we should break up."

What is sacrifice? Is it giving up a pleasure of life, be it personal or not and doing it for the sake of something greater? Yes, pretty much. I can sacrifice what I must. I have, for so long, for those who don't deserve it.

"You do realize I will not sleep tonight right? I can't sleep, not while knowing this time bomb is finally active. If you do not let me go now, not even what you are trying to save by saying 'I think' will calm me down."

"How do you think I feel? You believe that this is easy?"

"It's not that difficult. You made up your mind. I feel that you made it up a long time ago and decided just to bite your time until the perfect opportunity. I can tell."

I wanted to ask who 'he' was, as all my speculations of this inevitable phone call pointed towards that. Hell, even Samantha told me I might be a 'side guy', the term speaks for itself. But I was beyond this new X that will be just another person I wish I never met, just another waste of time. I knew, like so many others, she would try to stay friends with me because no one wants to carry ALL the guilt of breaking another person. 'We can stay friends' they say, like saying 'Your dog is dead, but you can keep it.'

"You have my number if you need anything. Maybe someday we'll be friends again."

"It will take time, K."

"… Can I at least get a 'someday'?"

"It. Will take. Time." *Click*

I hate knowing I can remember everything. The memory of meeting her for the first time is my new demon. I can never befriend an ex-girlfriend, any of them. What's the point? What's left? The friendship is clearly over once we agreed that we are more than just friends…

I can't be the only one who refuses to hold on to the memories, alone and saddened, the one who remembers the happiness and pretend everything is where it should be. I cannot grasp the concept that someone can decide to opt for taking the easy, cowardly way out instead of owning up to the possibility of breaking another person. I made a sacrifice for someone who didn't deserve it. Seven months worth of sacrificing destroyed in a 14-minute phone call. And we ask, "What's it all for?" But, time can be any length and instead of wasting it upset over something so trivial overall, staying friends wasn't a bad choice. I love knowing I still have so much to learn the way I handle situations and about myself. Sometimes, it just takes a while.

That was in January, and now we were in February. I was thinking of Sam, and there was no reason I shouldn't. I knew we were the best for each other because I have never known us to have a fight, a legitimate fight that results in us never speaking again. I honestly believed that if I asked her, and spoke of my thoughts of her, she might consider it. I have grown and perhaps grown to her exact liking. I knew I needed to tell her this soon but what was too soon? At the very least, I could start hinting at the idea and what luck, the day had just begun.

I thought of sending her a text but before long my family had come to visit and the day was far too young for the four of us to stay at home and to call it a day.

I love my family. They are the most important people in my life for I got the privilege of calling them my parents. There is still a little bit of confusion as to who the favorite child is, but upon closer examination, we realized because I was born first I get all the love.

They had always supported me in my times of need, and I can never repay their kindness except for being everything they wish for me to be.

After we had our family day and we were back home, the thought of her never escaped my mind. What would I say? How do I bring up the subject? It was as if I was going to meet her again for the first time. I was given a brand new canvas, and I was more than ready to paint my masterpiece.

As always, I never expect anything from her, much less, a call.
"Eyyy, what's up?"
"Sam! Hey, not much. Wow, a call? From you? Freaky."
"Haha, yeah! I'm having a few drinks right now."
"And what? No invite?"
"It with coworkers man. But hey, I have some news."
"Yeah? What's up?"

I expected a job promotion, or perhaps something funny that happened to her resulting in an amusing story. Hell, maybe she finally traded up for a new car and let her old Golf GT to rest. Sometimes, even I cannot prepare for the worst.

"I have a boyfriend now. It happened all random! Like, I have a boyfriend now, wei."

A Void In You

There is a face that can't be hidden.
It's a pain that boils on.
Every day is gloomy once more in this mind I call my home.
Here there was a grand solution; here I was a thought away. Here I begged for a tomorrow… and tomorrow came too late.
From the days we spend together, to the nights I shared, reborn.
Through a crowd here voice was healing, and I can hear it now… a very subtle, sweetened sound… It stings with harsh confusion.
I am left here once again…

…in thought.

Oh, the page, the page, forgive me…

…I have stained you in my red.
There's a pain that can't be hidden. It's a fate that came undone.
Every memory is rebuilding, every memory crashes down. Blackened days within horizons, those were never there before.
From the page to page just tell me what it was I fought you for…
Every day is now in memory… we can always be…

No more.

Click

"You wear your heart on your Sleeve." –Samantha

From the dark, in-between through the worlds own heart, stood in the tears a beautifully frightened image of the surface.

Through the watch, where in distance foreign leaves, drowning in the peace of all this loneliness of mine.

With a thought, with a hold straight through my faith, stood in the wake again every last color left unknown.

Although I pegged you for a dream, across is never seen when in emptiness, a mess.

And through these sorrows I have seen, believing in the gleam of a beauty worth the rest.

I want to dream. I wished to dream…

Leave me to dream, believe and see.

From the eyes, those saddened Phoenix eyes… in a final form of light I see it flying towards unknown.

As it cries, its precious form of flight keeps me in its sight that leaves me strong and yet so cold.

And through the undertone of dreams we're never as we seem, I begged for any chance.

And though I lived in no ones dream, where I became unseen was in everyone's distress.

But I want to dream… For I can be seen… Even in dreams of dreams of dreams.

I knew all your reason would keep me from feeling every single person's happiness.

And while I'm deceiving this worlds still believing every single step can't cleans the rest.

We all come back from our own dreams and only then it seems that sorrows aren't just tests.

And now these sorrows left unseen keep bleeding into dreams that only make a mess.

I want to dream. Please help me dream. Help me to dream of all the worlds unseen.

I want to dream… Let us both dream… Let us believe in dreams of peace.

April 4th, 2015

I've rewritten my words to show I've written them before.

    I walked passed her as I finished rewriting a song in my head, and while following my instincts I knew that she needed help, for she was a customer. I replayed it in my mind, after months of working here, that I will be the best I could be not because I needed to prove it to anyone, but because new jobs create new experiences.

The lessons never end.

    The unaccounted days and the fact that I finally, and perhaps for the last time, revisited that particular past filled me with New Harmony. I was no longer held back in my mind. I needed not to shame myself for the person I am.

I could finally move forward.

    I took into consideration that this person while in front of me could easily become another among the thousands I've met but could never actually meet. I became saddened at that thought for I wanted to meet her. I wanted to talk to her about anything that didn't have to do with this establishment and its overpriced attractions.
    I didn't know her and she didn't know me, but that didn't stop me from thinking she was so beautiful. With a simple glance into her eyes I knew she was someone I could hold meaningful conversations with, even if it were on something simple.
    Past experiences aside and without the need to blindly venture through an all too familiar environment, I did not let myself overthink a reality. I thought of treating her just as any other customer with kindness, a smile, perhaps a terrible joke and maybe even a discount if I could.
    I approached her. She was just in earshot distance and even before I could say a word, she beat me to it.
    "Hi." What a beautiful smile.

I may wear my heart on my sleeve, but I knew that someone out there did as well and maybe, just maybe I'd get the privilege of meeting her and what beautiful, coincidental luck, I got to meet her today.

www.ingramcontent.com/pod-product-compliance
Lightning Source LLC
LaVergne TN
LVHW041538060526
838200LV00037B/1045